Other books by

Losing Doll

American Tales

Reginald: A Tall Fish Tale
(a Children's Story)

This is a work of fiction. Names, characters, places and incidents either are the product of the author's imagination or are used fictitiously. Any resemblance to actual persons, live or dead, events or locales is entirely coincidental.

The Canal Murders

Murders

Ivan Joens

Chapter One

Near Edgware Road in London where the waters of the Regent's Canal tunnel below the street, a sidewalk dips to connect with the canal's towpath. Horses once trod this path pulling commercial canal boats against the slight current. The same canal boats, now brightly painted and converted for personal use, are moored in the canal end-to-end like dominos. In the near distance a bridge crosses the canal. Beside the bridge in a tangle of bushes and small trees sits the old Toll House, where the body was found.

It was the body of a young woman. It seems that it is always a young woman whose body is found in a secluded area. Men appear to prefer a public death: to be stabbed on the sidewalk outside a pub, shot in an angry encounter with a nut-job, or perish in the spasms of a heart attack in a busy cafe. Men seem to need immediate notice of their passing. Young women, however, too often die discreetly out of sight, unseen, secluded. Only later are they discovered. Everything changes when a young woman is involved.

The Toll House is a few short blocks from where I live. That morning I left for work at the usual time and walked towards the Tube station by way of the towpath. Ahead, a small group of people bunched in the middle of the path, blocking my way.

"There's a body," one of the men volunteered as I tried to walk around them. It seemed to give him great pleasure to relate the information. He turned from me to another man walking by and repeated it with a smile as if he couldn't believe his good luck.

The body had been discovered just minutes before by a tourist out early to photograph the Toll House in the gray light of the London morning. When I came to the scene he sat on the curb, looking sick. He told the small group gathered around him that the character of the building had attracted him. He had approached from the nearby bridge where he snapped a few shots then, leaving the bridge, he walked to the towpath for a closer view. However he was disappointed to find tall shrubbery which surrounded the structure obstructed his shot.

Fortunately a little-used path weaved through the tangle of bushes to an open space beside the building where he hoped to get a clear photo. This path was narrow and the uneven footing caused him to lurch and stumble over roots and rocks. A branch snagged and tore his suede jacket. Cursing, he angrily pulled away from it and fell, landing face to face with the dead woman.

A man in a business suit attempted to prevent curious onlookers from getting too near the body until the police arrived. From the tow-path I could see a single red shoe overturned in the rotting leaves and debris under the shrubs. It was one of those sexy, strappy styles of which young women are fond.

I was about to continue on my way — the man in the suit seemed to have the situation un-der control — when looking back from a differ-ent angle I could see the other red shoe. Near it a person's leg with its naked foot was visible under low-growing branches. The foot was bare but the leg was covered by fabric. I stopped cold. I recognized the fabric. Impossible not to remember, it was a particularly conspicuous print. A "statement print" is how she described it. Of course, another woman might own cloth-ing with the same print but I knew life doesn't work like that. If you think something terrible is about to overcome you, it generally does. I needed to see her face to be certain.

The man in the suit who took his job seriously stopped me when I attempted to look at the body.

"Please move on, no need for gawking," he said tersely as I approached him.

"I believe I may know her."

"Right, I've heard that one already. Move along."

"No! I may be able to identify her. I'm afraid this is a coworker of mine. If it isn't, I will be on my way."

"Let him have a look. He says he knows her. He shouldn't have to wait to find out," said the first man, still smiling at all this good luck.

"Go on then, but for God's sake man, simply look, do not touch or disturb anything."

Twisting my way nervously along the path I reached the body. It lay on its side under branches of the hedge. The branches near her body had been broken. The body's position was unnatural. It was obvious that she had not fallen there; she had been dumped. The face was turned to the left, facing me. When the photographer tripped and fell, he stared directly into those cold dead eyes.

It was my friend. And it wasn't. It was unquestionably her body but in death it was no longer the woman I had known. An image made of wax or clay, modeled in her shape and with her features perhaps, but not her person. I responded as I might to a death in a movie. It wasn't real. The woman I knew would be at the office when I arrived. Before me was a shape like hers but it could not actually be her. It was something else, something with her bloodless face, her contorted body, her statement clothes, but it was not her. That's how they do it in the movies, they counterfeit the details. It all looks so real and then the lights come up, the credits roll and the film ends. But this one didn't end. It refused to be a movie.

I waited beside the slow-moving waters of the canal for the police to arrive. An empty paper cup drifted with the flow, slid along the hull

of a canal boat and disappeared under the sur-
face of the canal water.

Chapter Two

We met at a pub after work to chat, as usual. However, this time no one spoke. The murder of someone you know, but are not close to, can seem random and purposeless. To be honest, we don't care much if a stranger is murdered. We might wonder, what is this world coming to? However, we don't respond and the memory doesn't linger. On the other hand, when a family member is killed we take it personally. It wounds, it angers. We want revenge: we demand justice. A co-worker is different, between the two extremes. We know them; we have lunched, perhaps argued, endured meetings together but we are not emotionally connected. Their murder leaves us feeling suspended, slowly spinning, hoping at some point to get our feet back on the ground.

I held a pint of beer, soothed by the feel of the glass, cold and smooth, wet from condensation. I watched my thumb as I swiped at the moisture, leaving a path. To my right Paul absently flicked at his smart phone. He hadn't touched his beer. Across the table from me Rita had moved in her chair to study her nails. Turning her hand over, palm up, she curled her fingers so the nails faced her. Each nail was examined then the polish was tested with her thumb. Her other hand raised a vodka sour each time a nail passed inspection. That left Ellie.

"This is a total waste of time. We should be doing something useful."

Paul stopped flicking. "Like what? Writing our names on a card to her? Sleuthing? Lot of good that will do. I could be sitting on a clue and wouldn't know it. Let the police do their job."

She looked at him without speaking until he turned his attention back to his phone then she spoke. "Did it occur to you that we may know the killer?"

His head snapped up, "What?"

"She was alive when we all left Neal's farewell dinner last night. Possibly it was one of the people there."

"Are you serious? That's impossible. Why would someone in our office want to kill Samantha? Everyone liked her. Nothing unusual happened at the dinner. It was the standard, obligatory, boring farewell dinner. Nothing but endless speeches that no one listened to or cared about."

"And yet she was murdered later."

"That doesn't mean it was one of us. Perhaps she was robbed on her way home or got into a fight with a boyfriend. Could have been anyone. How do you even know she was murdered? Perhaps it was an accident."

"What do you think?" Ellie asked me, holding eye contact with me a little too long I thought.

"It wasn't a robbery; the police found her wallet in the shrubs while I was talking to the Inspector. Cash and credit cards were still in it. Also, it was no accident. I could see blood soaking her blouse when they moved the body but there was no blood on the ground. My guess is that she was killed elsewhere and her body was dumped there by the canal."

"Didn't have a boyfriend, did she?" asked Rita still examining her fingers.

While Ellie continued to stare at me Paul answered, "No, I teased her about that. Told her she would end up with a house full of cats if she did not meet someone soon. She told me she was happy being single, and that she loved cats. She seemed to think that was particularly funny." This memory seemed to get the better of his emotions for a moment, his eyes glistened.

Without looking at me Rita asked, "Do the police suspect you, what with knowing her, being with her the night before and finding the body and all?"

I flinched but replied, "I am sure that they suspect everyone who was at our dinner last night...including you." I had to add that last bit, partly out of spite for reminding me that I was indeed a suspect and partly to get a reaction from her. Rita and I were certainly not best friends.

"Hmph, damned foolish if they do." She finished her drink, stood and left us without a glance. I didn't know if she was angry or just being Rita. It was hard for me to tell the difference.

"Bit awkward, that. Well, it is time I should go too. Be sure to tell me when you solve this case, Inspector Ellie," Paul said with a smile to her.

She returned his smile as he left us at the table.

"Now what?" she asked me.

I continued to stare out the door of the pub after watching Paul leave through it, consciously looking away from Ellie. She knew something. I could either act like I had no idea what she was talking about or I could trust her and tell her what I knew. I decided that I was not ready to do either, just yet.

"I have to leave too, Ellie, but how about if we meet at my neighborhood pub tomorrow at six, if you don't already have a commitment." I felt certain that she would decline. As attractive as she was, surely she would have a Saturday night date.

"Where the dinner was held last night? The scene of the crime as it were?" She stood, put on her jacket and said, "Yes, let's do that. I shall meet you there." She held out her hand. Rising, I shook hands with her, realizing as I did so that this was more than a handshake, she was inviting me to join her and we were entering into a sort of compact, one that might take us places we didn't want to go.

Chapter Three

Three blocks from the Regent's Canal in my neighborhood stands The Crown. As pubs go it is typical. The front door opens to a large room with high ceilings. Tables, booths and bar stools clutter the space. In the center is a three-sided bar projecting from the rear wall. A door beside the bar leads outside to a back patio enclosed by tall brick walls. A half dozen picnic-style tables are scattered throughout the space.

Behind the bar is a small office with a door that opens onto a hallway used by suppliers to bring beer in the side door from the alley.

Kegs of beer are wheeled through the hallway to the basement. Up one level from the bar is a dining area, cozy with low ceilings. The top floor is the residence of the pub's manager, Will, who frequently tends bar and leaves for parts unknown every Tuesday and Wednesday. In front of the building sit small bistro tables for customers to interact with passers-by on the sidewalk, many of whom are neighbors that stop and chat. A locally owned grocery store to the right, a butcher's shop to the left and a wine shop across the street serve the eating and drinking needs of the community.

I made a practice of stopping daily at The Crown on my way home after work. It was a pleasant way to meet neighbors and was preferable to going home to my empty flat. Because the pub was centrally located and the food was unusually good we had selected it for Neal's farewell dinner on Thursday night.

Two nights later, on Saturday, I walked from my flat to meet Ellie there. As I neared the pub I saw Will smile sadly to welcome me while clearing the tables in front.

"I was sorry to hear about your friend. Tragic. Nasty business. My condolences." He shook my hand and held it in his. "That abso- lutely lovely young lady who was here for the dinner party is inside." He leaned towards me confidentially, "Said she is waiting for you. Asked for you by name, she did. She and her two lady friends have brightened things here considerably. Please do tell me if there is any- thing I can do for you."

"Thank you. Two lady friends with her? Tell me, do you also remember them from the other night?"

"Possibly, but to be honest, your particular lady friend," (here he paused significantly) "tends to be most memorable."

"Come in with me so I can introduce you."

"Oh no, no, no. Thank you but no, Join your friends. I have more tidying to do."

Inside, I immediately spotted the table where Ellie and the two women were seated.

"Hope you don't mind, " Ellie said, "I invited Ilyse and Valerie to join us. They may have ideas or perhaps noticed something that will help us."

"Of course I don't mind. More ideas are most welcome," I smiled in greeting my co-workers. "I hope you can help because I cannot imagine who or why anyone would want to hurt Samantha."

"We all were shocked, of course," Ellie said. "I told them that you and I want to do what we can and they want to help us."

Ilyse and Valerie, like me, were expats. Although born and raised in Germany, Ilyse's command of American English was better than mine. She had attended a language school and mastered an American accent so perfectly that I had mistaken her for American when I joined the office.

There was no mistaking where Valerie was from, her French accent was thick but charming. Aware that we had difficulty under-standing her, she spoke in short, direct sen-tences. Even so it was sometimes difficult to

18

comprehend her. It took me weeks to understand what city in France she was from. "The
city of Samalo, on the coast," she had answered
when I asked. Later, I searched for it on a map,
gave up, tried again one morning in the office a
week or two later and got the same answer.

"In what province is Samalo?" I asked
hoping to narrow it down a little.

"Brittany, of course." she had answered,
as if every school child who paid attention in
geography class should know that.

Ilyse whose desk was nearby had come to
my rescue, "I believe Americans pronounce all
the letters, like in 'Saint Louis.' Got it?"

I didn't know what St. Louis had to do with
Samalo.

She tried again, "Perhaps you pronounce it
'Saint Malo'?"

St. Malo! Of course I knew of it. A daily
ferry sailed there from the English coast. And of
course the French pronunciation was more fluid
and sexy than the American. Valerie did not un-

derstand my confusion and had been guarded with me thereafter.

As I joined them at the table I noticed that the pub was unusually quiet. Looking around I realized our table was the center of attention. No matter that Valerie and Ilyse are young and attractive women and a majority of the pub's customers were men, all eyes were on Ellie. For good reason; she is simply stunning. An exotic combination of ethnic backgrounds she turns every head wherever she goes.

I suggested that we move to the back patio for more privacy but Ilyse said, "I think we will be fine here. I've been out with Ellie before and you know what? Everyone just looks, no one ever bothers her. It's like they are afraid of her. When Valerie and I go out guys chat us up but if Ellie comes along they stay away and just stare. Odd isn't it?"

The front door was pulled open with difficulty and in tottered Stephen, the pub's mascot-like drunk. The door swept him into the room, his feet taking him one way, his arms and head going another. Aiming for a chair at the bar, he missed badly and seemed on a collision course with our table. However Will had followed him in and with a firm grip on the back of his collar had steered him to a safe landing in an empty booth near us.

Very sleight and wiry, Stephen was not much larger than a child. With a head-full of white hair I guessed his age was somewhere between sixty and eighty; he was always drunk so it was hard to be certain. His routine was unchanging: each evening he would make his unsteady entrance, sing songs that no one recognized until finally someone would buy him a drink. When his glass was empty the singing would resume and the cycle would be repeated until eventually he would quietly pass out.

Will propped him up in the booth where he looked around the room apparently trying to remember where he was. Then he saw Ellie.

"Hoo. Dis laymen 'rold simmen wud hem!"

Stephen may have been speaking Welch, Dutch or English. No one seemed to know for sure.

The women looked to me for a translation.

"I think that means he likes you," I said to Ellie. Ilyse dissolved in laughter. "Let's go talk with him, Val. Maybe he will 'simmen wud' with us!" They joined him in his booth, Ilyse speaking German, Valerie French while Stephen smiled happily at them and interjected his unintelligible comments.

"I asked them to join us tonight" Ellie said to me, smiling when Ilyse reached across the booth to prevent Stephen from slipping under it. "I hope you don't mind. I thought we could all talk about our Thursday night dinner. Perhaps putting our heads together will help us remember something."

Stephen's high tenor broke into song. After the first chorus and using the table to help him stand he attempted to bow before Ilyse, perhaps to ask her to dance, however by inclining his head he lost his balance, tilted forward, caught himself before falling on her in the booth but overcompensated and suddenly found himself sitting on the floor.

"Whoosh, hun trondle foll ren, fligage!" he said with dignity as he sadly looked around. Aware that he could not stand Stephen remained helplessly on the floor with his legs straight out in front of him. He looked like a toy that had fallen from a shelf.

I lifted him to his feet. While I held him steady, he smiled again at Ilyse and Valerie, ready to resume his courting. Will touched my shoulder, "perhaps we should put him in the back booth for now." We guided him to a booth beside the door to the patio. I propped him in the corner while Will got him a drink. With the drink in front of him, I left him there reasonably sure that he wouldn't go far.

"So sad," Valerie said looking over at him.

"Was he here that night?" asked Ellie.

"He is here every night but I doubt that he remembers it." I replied.

"I know but I think if we remember every-thing that we can from that night while it is fresh in our memories we might uncover a clue that will help. Let's start with who was here."

"Right, well, we had two tables for six up-stairs in the dining room so there were twelve of us. Obviously Neal, the guest of honor, was there. Samantha, who he always liked, sat to his right. Then there was Rita, me and Paul. Vince, who of course had to make his usual inane speech, sat to his left."

"At our table Valerie and I sat next to each other," Ilyse remembered. "Ellie was across the table beside the twins. James sat between us. That was everyone."

"Non," Valerie shook her head, "not every-one. There was the stranger."

"The stranger? Who was that?" I asked.

"That's right!" Ellie added. "Your friend, remember? He joined us late. You and Saman-tha knew him."

"Hugh?" I asked.

"Oui, Hugh. That is the man I remember."

"True, he joined us but he only stayed for a few minutes."

Valerie nodded, "This thing however, I noticed." She waited for someone to ask her what she noticed.

"What was it?" Ellie kindly asked.

"The jealousy. Neal had the jealousy. It was evident."

"Now that she mentions it, I noticed his response too," Ilyse said. "Neal reacted very oddly when you introduced Hugh to the rest of us. He positively glared at Samantha."

"He did? Are you sure, Valerie? Maybe he was reacting to something she said."

"No. I am certain. Of this there can be no doubt. He had the jealousy."

We considered what the implications might be if he was angry with Samantha. However, we would not get any answers from Neal. He had flown to Hong Kong the day after his dinner to manage our office there.

"What do we do? Should we tell the police?" asked Ilyse.

"Let's see what else we can come up with first. What else do you remember?"

"Well, I noticed that the twins left very early," I volunteered, glad to have something to contribute.

Ilyse giggled.

"Why is that funny?"

"Did you notice anyone else leave early?"

"No, not really. Why?"

"Because Valerie and I left with them! We went clubbing." she laughed.

"Apparently I am not observant," I admitted. I had been talking with Hugh when I noticed that the twins were missing. "There was another person who I remember was there — the server."

"That cute Australian man," Ilyse agreed. "How did I forget him? He seemed so shy and hardly spoke but he was adorable. Unlikely suspect, but he was there. That's everyone. Like Paul said yesterday, the dinner was boring. Nothing else happened." No one disagreed. The table became silent.

"Alright then, if we have no one else to add and no great ideas, Val and I are going back to that club. OK?"

"Go on, if we think of anything I'll call you," Ellie waved them away. I started to leave too. "You, stay," she said holding my arm. "You and I have more to talk about." Still holding my arm she waited until they left through the front door and walked past the window in the direction of the Underground. "We both need a drink, would you mind getting them?"

I ordered at the bar, waited for the drinks and placed them on the table, trying to read her face. "Cheers!" she said, we touched glasses and each took a healthy swallow.

"I know," she whispered, holding her glass at eye level.

"You know what?"

"About you and Samantha."

Chapter Four

I considered acting like I didn't know what she was talking about but I remembered our handshake, the implicit agreement that we had entered into. If she knew about me and Samantha there was no point in denying it. All the same, I was afraid of what she might know.

"I know everything. I know she liked you very much. I know you were sleeping together. I know all about your relationship. I am afraid I know more about it than you do."

"Sam told you?"

"She did."

"I admit I am surprised. She was the one who wanted it to be a secret. Office gossip and all that. She insisted that we not tell anyone. I can't believe she told you."

Yesterday morning when I saw her body lying under the tangled branches I went numb. I refused to believe it. The scene must have been staged. It wasn't Sam. It couldn't be. I told myself she was still alive. It hadn't happened. I couldn't believe it and tried to block it out.

I guess I thought that if no one knew about our relationship then the private world we had created would continue, the private world filled with Sam. The one where she was still alive.

But now that Ellie knew about us everything changed. That world which Sam and I shared had been breached. The real world was breaking down the door, making me accept the truth, the truth I had tried so hard to deny.

Ellie reached across the table and squeezed my hand. In that instant Sam died.

The blood I had seen on her blouse was real blood, her blood. Those dead, unmoving eyes were her eyes. She was gone. Denying it wouldn't change that. I finished my drink, feeling cold and thirsty and empty and angry.

"I am so sorry. I can't imagine what you went through, seeing her like that. I can't think how difficult it was for you."

"It has become much more difficult. I am sorry, it is getting to me now." I felt like I had been falling for days and had finally cratered onto the ground.

She patted the back of my hand. I went away. I was with Sam. We were alone on Hugh's canal boat, having tea on the stern. The setting was almost magical. With a nearby Anglican church as the backdrop, the canal water slowly tapping at the boat's hull and the intensity of Sam's person beside me I felt outside time and place. There was nothing else. Only us. She took my tea cup and snuggled close while we dreamed that we owned the boat and were about to embark, like river gypsies, for places unknown. I was with her again.

"I need to tell you something else." Ellie brought me back, her hand on my arm again.

I waited, not wanting to leave Sam and the boat.

"I need to tell you why Samantha told me about your relationship. She wanted my advice. You see ..." She drank deeply from her glass, "I have to tell you the truth even though I know this will hurt you. Sam came to me because her life had become complicated." She paused again. Then, finishing her drink Ellie went on, "She asked for my help. You see, Sam was having a relationship with someone else at the same time she was seeing you."

The moment Ellie told me I realized that I had known all along. There was always that re-serve, that little bit held back. Nothing concrete. Just a feeling. Not enough to risk confronting her. Upsetting her if I was wrong. Now it didn't matter at all because she was gone.

"You alright?" Ellie looked concerned.

"Yeah, I guess I suspected something. Do you know who he is?"

"She."

"She what?"

"Her lover was a she. A woman. Like I said Sam's life was complicated."

A woman? Sam told me about previous men in her life but never said anything about liking women. I tried to remember, did I know anyone that she would be attracted to? Possibly someone at work; someone who is exotically beautiful?

"Was it you, Ellie?"

She had expected the question. Her hand remained on my arm. "At one time, before you, we were close. But it wasn't me. She never told me who it was, only that she had known her for a long time and was torn between you and her."

"When was this? When did she come to you for advice?"

"About two weeks ago, not long. She hated deceiving both of you and knew that she had to decide. That's why she came to me. She wanted me to help her make a decision. I told her that I would listen and try to help her sort her feelings but she had to make the choice."

"Did she? Had she decided?"

"I don't know. When we talked about it last week she was torn in two. Sorry, I wish I knew so I could tell you."

Gradually the noise in the pub had returned. Conversations had resumed; in his booth Stephen was inert, for the present. Outside, it was light but the day was fading.

"I think I'd like to be alone."

"I understand, but do me a favor first? Walk with me to the Underground by way of the Toll House?" Ellie asked.

"You want to see where she was found?"

"Yes, would you mind?"

I never wanted to see that place again. A mental image of it was branded in my memory. It was the last place on earth I wanted to go, yet I owed it to Sam to try to learn what happened.

We walked the few blocks from the Pub to the canal, turned right on the towpath and stopped at the scene. I pointed out the path through the hedges with the Toll House in the background. The ground where Sam had been found near the red shoes had been raked clean.

"C'mon then, let's have a look," she said but instead of taking the path she walked to the bridge over the canal. At the middle of the bridge, directly above the canal, Ellie stopped. The view from here was very scenic with multi-colored canal boats lying on both sides of the canal, tranquil and picturesque. She pointed to an area beside the Toll House.

"Look…" Ellie pointed, "…there. I am sure that is where she was pulled into the hedges, from the canal side not the street side. The killer didn't use the path. The street lights would have exposed him to people passing by on the sidewalk or the road. Also, anyone looking from one of the houses that line the street beside the canal could have seen them on the path. It would have been too exposed. Our killer brought the body by boat and dumped it using the shrubbery to cover his movements. The canal side would have been dark and hidden from view except for anyone standing where we are."

"That makes sense. The path is too narrow and uneven; it would have been nearly impossible for anyone to carry a body on it especially in the dark. I could hardly see well enough to squeeze through the branches in daylight. I agree, it had to be someone using a canal boat."

"Not necessarily a canal boat; other types of boats are permitted on the canals too. Possibly a row boat, it would be quieter and less conspicuous than a canal boat." Twilight muted the colors of the gaily painted boats before us. Slowly, floating with the current, geese emerged from under the bridge, dipping their heads as they fed. "Didn't you say your friend, Hugh, lives on a canal boat when you introduced him at the dinner?"

"He does; it is moored a block from here in that direction," I pointed behind us.

Not far at all from where Sam had been dumped like rubbish.

Chapter Five

I'm a pretty normal guy. I'm intelligent enough to keep up with most of my friends and have usually done pretty well at whatever I try. I don't fail often but when I do, it doesn't bother me; I believe it's bound to happen occasionally and when it does I'm not worried what people will say or think about me. I'm not thin-skinned so I take criticism in stride.

All of this helped me handle it when Ellie told me Sam had another lover. It didn't affect me the way it might some people. My ego wasn't bruised and I didn't feel any jealousy. I accepted that the very things I loved about Sam could also lead her to love someone else. Her energy, her tenderness and her joy couldn't be constrained. It was bound to happen sooner or later.

What I could not accept was having her life taken from her. Seeing her broken body lying in the shrubbery, with her dead eyes staring at nothing, had numbed me. I didn't feel pain or even sadness at the time. In fact, I didn't feel anything. I went through the motions, walking and talking, but I wasn't present.

I was still in that state when Ellie confronted me about my relationship with Sam and woke me from it.

The same thing had happened to me once before: in college an uncle called to tell me my father had been wounded in a random LA freeway shooting. He survived the bullet but was never the same.

I took a break from college to be with him at the hospital. The tedium of sitting beside his hospital bed, while he lay unresponsive but alive, left me with the same numb sensation that

Sam's murder had. When he got better I slowly came back to life, hoping every day that the police would tell us they had a lead in the case. They never did; the shooter got away with it.

After college I worked for a year in downtown Los Angeles to stay near my family. Then, I took a job in Seattle. I took it, even though it meant leaving my family behind. A new job, a new city, maybe I could get back on track.

Seattle helped. I worked hard and enjoyed it. Promotions followed and by the time I turned thirty I was doing well enough to be offered a position on the Regional Management Team in London.

I accepted the offer, although it seemed like I was giving up on Dad. In Seattle there was at least a chance I might stumble across a clue related to Dad's case. That wouldn't happen in London.

I knew, deep down, it wouldn't have happened in Seattle either. I had been kidding myself because I wanted to feel like I was doing something. I wasn't. I stopped kidding myself, moved to London and, there, I met Sam.

***

Boats played an important role in my relationship with her. It seemed likely that a boat may have been involved in taking her from me. Earlier it was one that brought us together.

In late spring, I had moved to London. I was busy learning my new job, getting to know my coworkers and adjusting to a climate with even more rainy days than Seattle when the boss, Vince, announced he had arranged a Thames river cruise for a Friday night office party to kick off a series of sales campaigns we were launching. The boat ride itself was terrific. There was plenty of liquor, a great DJ and priceless nighttime scenery as our boat cruised for three hours up and down the Thames through the beautifully lit buildings, bridges and monuments of London. The boat discharged us, drunk and amped up, near a Tube station beside the Thames, where according to Vince's plan, we would all board trains on the Underground and journey safely home. However, it is virtually impossible for sixty party-goers to shut down that quickly. Various groups spread out to continue the party at a few nearby pubs.

I don't think Samantha and I intended to end up in the same group. It wasn't as if we had been eyeing each other in the office. Of course I had noticed her; we worked together after all. I suppose we're both considered attractive, but so were a number of people in the office. I was attracted to Sam because she was quick-witted and tart. She livened up meetings at the office, but it was her high energy that appealed because it never flagged, daylong.

Coming off the boat, more than a little drunk, she carried nine or ten of us in her wake to a pub where we continued drinking until slowly the others peeled off leaving me and Samantha side by side. Even before they left I felt us coming together because, well, we should, like the gin and tonic she tasted of when we kissed out-side the pub. No seduction or romance was in-volved; we left together and went to my place without making small talk, without second thoughts, without turning on the lights, without clothes, without sleeping, until Saturday dawned on us.

Lying full-length, facing me, without any covering, she rested her head on her hand, "Now what?" she asked.

Unprepared, I hadn't expected to answer questions about our relationship. I stammered, "I, uh, really like you a lot."

She howled, I absolutely cracked her up. Tears ran from her eyes.

"You are a hoot, aren't you? No, that's not what I meant, although I like you too, especially your cute chin. I meant what shall we do? I am not ready to go home yet. I want to go out and do something fun this morning."

Relieved, I suggested "There's a cafe down the street where we could have breakfast." She waited for something a little more active. I thought fast, "Or we could walk by the canal to Camden Town."

"Camden Town!" her eyes lit up. Then a question crossed her face, "where the hell am I? I didn't pay attention on the Tube last night. We did ride the Tube didn't we?"

I explained where she was and that it was only a block to the canal but the walk to Camden Town wasn't short. It would take us through a warehouse area to Regent's Park where we would pass behind the mansions and then past the zoo before we got to it. It was at least a couple miles.

"What are we waiting for? I love Camden."

We stopped for coffee, then walked on the towpath beside the old Toll House. Canal boats were moored on both sides of the canal up to the tunnel under Edgware Road. Like me, Samantha was taken by their charm. Compared to air travel or racing along motorways in a car, the idea of floating across the countryside of

England seemed relaxing and sedate. The tang of coal smoke lay low on the canal.

"I love that smell, reminds me of my gran. They use it in their stoves?" she asked.

"Most do, I think. There is one farther along that burns wood. Smells like a campfire in the middle of London. It would be fun to have a canal boat."

"You mean a narrow boat, that's what they 're called. You should buy one! It would be brilliant!"

We admired the narrow boats and then walked past the warehouses, the park and the zoo before preparing ourselves for the onslaught of people in Camden Town which hit us like opening the gates at a rock concert. A hive of bodies shopping and selling, buildings impaled by attention-attracting plaster rockets and more colors than a kaleidoscope. It was like stepping into a comic book with a loud rock soundtrack. Music was everywhere, in the stores, over the sidewalks and on the streets. Samantha mainlined the energy. It was in her blood, her eyes beamed. At that moment she was the happiest human being I had ever seen. She radiated it to all the people around us. They joined her, she joined them and I lost her to the experience. Before dancing away, she ran back and kissed me still tasting of gin and was gone.

That was the pattern for our relationship.

After that we spent weekends together, Sam going full speed, me holding on for dear life, enjoying the ride.

Chapter Six

He had not intended to kill. That part of his fantasy was not planned. He had resolved to find a spot where he could grab a young girl undetected. Location was everything. It needed to be near a school or playground but in an isolated place outside of London where no one would witness the grab. When he found it that sparkling spring afternoon the situation had presented itself so perfectly, so much like he had envisioned in his fantasies, that he promptly acted. She was alone below the school grounds, her attention glued to an app on her phone and only a short distance from his automobile. Coming up from behind he put one hand over her mouth and with the other around her waist, lifted her. The action was so unexpected that he had carried her some steps toward the car before she began to struggle. His hand continued to cover her mouth after he put her roughly in the trunk. Making a fist he threatened to punch her while removing his hand from her mouth. She barely had a moment to scream before he closed the trunk lid. Then the screams were only faintly audible. He quickly looked about to see if they were still alone.

They were not.

Two girls coming over the hill above had seen him. One looked directly at him. She reminded him of his mother. Younger but it was the face of his mother. She began to scream. His mother screamed. He hated screaming. The other girl ran down the hill towards him, running very fast like a little demon. He was in the car speeding away before she got near.

The girls might have seen his face but if so, it was from a distance and he was confident that his license number hadn't been visible from their vantage.   After a quarter mile he slowed, now was not the time to be stopped for speeding.   Screaming continued from the trunk but he was able to drown it with the car radio.   Fortunately he had plenty of gas and could drive to his destination without stopping.

His fantasy had not included her terror when he finally stopped the car in the countryside.   It absolutely ruined it for him.   Trying to calm her had only made it worse. He tried to be gentle but like a feral cat she bit, scratched and continued that incessant screaming.   It made him crazy. He had to stop it. Shouting at her didn't work, pleading didn't.   She might have stopped if he hit her but he couldn't do that. He wasn't that kind of man. His hand on her throat finally made the screaming stop.   It resumed however when he removed his hand so he had no choice but to make her stop again. The quiet when he put his hand on her throat was the quiet he had imagined in his fantasy.   In it he was firm but gentle and affectionate and she was complaisant, demure. Why did things never turn out the way you hoped they would? You could plan, you could dream; no matter, in the end disappointment would result. This quiet after the screaming was bliss. She lay there now like a perfect little angel. Her eyes had been terrible for the last few moments. Now he closed them.

***

He hadn't considered how to dispose of a body. His admittedly incomplete planning hadn't included such a contingency. Pulling her body out of the car and abandoning her on the bare ground seemed too cruel. Scavenging animals might desecrate her remains. No, his little angel deserved better than that but what other choices were there? Burying her would be difficult — he didn't have tools, it would take too much time and, besides, was it even possible to bury an angel?

No, she needed space in the open air where she could transition to her new spirit form without impediments. He remembered a painting of Ophelia at the Tate, floating blissfully down river, serenely dead. Serenity is what she deserved. However he couldn't risk driving to a river — none were within twenty miles — and certainly not with the body of a young girl in the trunk. The only waterway nearby was the Grand Canal. If he drove slowly using little traveled roads he could be there in ten minutes. Dusk was at hand. He would quickly put her in the water and be gone.

He knew just the place. He had fished from the towpath there once. Hadn't caught anything but it was easy to drive to. The only shortcoming was that it was in sight of a busy roadway but dusk should screen him and the motorway made for a quick get-away. He stopped his car beside the canal. It was deserted, as he had hoped, no fishermen remained at day's end.

Opening the trunk he carried her to the canal putting her feet in first. As he slowly released her into the water he realized this wouldn't work. She would sink, not float. He pulled her out and laid her beside the canal. With the last bit of dusk reflected in the water he looked at her lying on her side in thick grass which grew beside the canal; she seemed almost content. He arranged her hair. Better, but something still wasn't right. In a flash of inspiration, he removed her wet shoes. There! Barefoot like one of the seraphim she appeared before him. No beast would dare disturb such a godly creature.

He stroked her hair for a moment and kissed the top of her head before starting the engine of his car and joining the motorway traffic.

Chapter Seven

Three nights after the Thames cruise, still alive with the excitement of my new relationship with Sam, I sat on the rear patio of my pub while rain threatened to chase me inside. I was alone except for another man who sat with his back to me at a table against the wall. Standing when the first rain drops began to fall, his chair scraped loudly on the concrete.

"Sorry," he said, heading for the door.

"No worries. Giving it up, are you?"

He turned back to me, "Giving it up?"

"Yes, giving in to the rain. Going inside."

"Ah, yes. Indeed I am. Surely you don't intend to sit alone in the rain, do you? How very sad that would be."

The rain picked up so I followed him inside. "Join me for a pint?" I asked.

"Actually I had planned to return to my boat for the evening but thank you. Perhaps next time," he answered. I could see him better now. He appeared to be in his mid-forties and slender with greying hair. About my height, six foot.

"Returning to your boat, you said?"

"Yes, I live on my narrow boat not many blocks from here."

"That is a coincidence. My friend was just telling me I should buy one. She thought it would be fun."

"Don't listen to her. They are rubbish. Cramped, expensive — the upkeep is constant, no privacy to speak of. Terrible idea. Perhaps I will see you again, accept the pint you offered and tell you more reasons that it is a bad idea. It is a frightfully long list." He stuck out his hand,

"My name is Hugh." After completing the usual formalities of introducing ourselves he left and I found a space at the bar on the opposite side of the pub from where Stephen had broken into song. I wasn't ready to go back to my flat. It was too easy there to fall into reading work related emails which always lead to doing work and I did enough of that during the day. That was the problem with being employed by a global company, there was always someone somewhere in the world who was up and working and sending me emails. When the work day was over I wanted to relax and no better way to do that then at the Crown. The goings-on were free entertainment and when there was a lull I could talk to Will behind the bar.

"Have you ever thought of living on a narrow boat, Will?" I asked, taking a barstool next to a regular who always wore the same brown sweater.

"No, I wouldn't fancy that. Cottage in the country is what I would want. Perhaps some sheep. Someplace quiet and cozy. Why do you ask? Will you be buying one?"

"I met a man on the patio who lives on one. Got me thinking."

"You met Hugh, did you? Nice chap. Lucky sod, bleeding money."

Hugh hadn't struck me as being wealthy but then I've heard that the ones who seem wealthy usually aren't so maybe the converse was also true. For some reason it made me trust him; a guy who is loaded but chooses to live on a rather humble boat is all right by me.

Will left me to take care of a customer. I decided it was time to leave, more customers had entered the pub and Will would be occupied for some time. He saw me gathering my things and said over his shoulder to me, "Be careful going home. I have heard stories that some people have been roughed up after dark."

"Robbed?"

"Perhaps, I don't know. Better to be alert."

I was surprised. It didn't seem like the neighborhood for crime. Deep pockets are required to buy property here. The only reason I can afford my flat is our company has a generous housing allowance for expats. After Will's warning I was particularly alert walking home in the dark. I decided to follow a woman with two children. I told myself that I was looking out for them and providing protection, like I was a bodyguard or something, yet I felt exposed and vulnerable when they turned and climbed the steps to their building. Being alone in a city of more than eight million people can make you feel that way.

The street was abnormally quiet. My footsteps echoed dully off the buildings. No dogs barked. No car doors slammed. Ominously a hallway light in the building next to me went out the same moment as did a front room light across the street. Soundlessly the blinking lights of an aircraft moved across the sky. The silence seemed oppressive and made me nervous but when a bus roared down a nearby street I worried that the noise would mask the sound of someone coming up behind me. When the noise passed I welcomed the return of silence.

My building was a half block ahead. Thankfully the front light was on. I removed my keys from my pocket, promptly dropped them on the sidewalk, cussed, bent over and picked them up. When I stood I saw movement in front of my building. Maybe a person, maybe not. A breeze blowing the branches of the tree in front? Could be, but the air was calm where I stood. I decided to cross the street and look at it from a different perspective hoping my imagination was playing tricks on me.

I took my time, walking slowly and watching intently but nothing moved. Finally across the street from the front door I stopped and stared into the darkness all around me. Confident at last that I had been imagining things I walked up the steps, unlocked and opened the door. When I heard a rush of sound behind me, I quickly stepped inside and locked the door behind me. Safely behind the door I listened intently but the sound had stopped.

***

I waited the next night for Sam outside a restaurant in Soho. Standing there, I realized that meeting Sam on a Saturday evening in Soho was probably not a wise idea. A riot of people spilled over the sidewalks onto the streets. Many were already drunk and the re-mainder appeared hellbent on catching up with them. Dinner and a show had seemed like a solid date night plan. I knew she wouldn't enjoy sitting through a drama so I purchased tickets to a rock musical. Dinner a few blocks away seemed like a no-brainer but I hadn't counted on the bedlam in Soho. Since Sam wasn't terribly disciplined when it came to appointments I had reminded her at lunch to meet me here. When I got to Soho I called her to warn her about the crowds (to be honest, I called to remind her again of our date).

She was outside the tube station she said but Sam was an unabashed and unapologetic liar. She didn't lie to be devious but to "make people happy." Her rational was that events would turn out the same whether or not she lied so she might as well tell the person what they wanted to hear and they'd feel better in the meantime. Really when you thought about it, she reasoned, lying to them was a considerate gesture. She was completely without guilt.

I worried that the odds of her getting from Piccadilly Tube station to our Soho restaurant might only be about fifty-fifty. The distractions en route were formidable. Although she was a designer by trade and quite smart she readily admitted that she was easily distracted by shiny things. Between the people partying in the streets and the retail shops on Shaftesbury Ave. who knew where she might end up?

I realized much too late that I should have met her at the station and brought her in hand to dinner with me. Now there was no remedy. I couldn't call her again without appearing not to trust her and there was nothing that cute little liar disliked more than not being trusted. I paced nervously doubting she would show. After waiting for some time it appeared that she had been sidetracked and that I should consider going to the theatre to find buyers for the tickets. Then out of the hundreds of people on the sidewalks in front of me I saw her smiling face walking towards me. She wore a white top (her concession to our "formal" date night), fire-engine red slacks (mirrored on her cheeks) and hiking boots which asserted that she was still her own person, damn the fashion industry. Seeing her made my heart pound.

We talked at dinner although I gladly did most of the listening. At the theatre she screamed and cheered and sang along with the cast - I thought she was much more entertaining than the show. Afterwards, on the way to my flat we stopped at The Crown for a few drinks. Hugh was sitting at the first table inside the door. He recognized me immediately, saw Sam then stood to say hello. By way of introduction I said, "Hugh, may I introduce you to Sam, the young lady who recommended I buy a narrow boat? And Sam, Hugh is the owner of a narrow boat who said it would be a mistake to buy one."

"Worse! It would be positively daft! Pleased to meet you Sam. Please, join me." He waved us to chairs at his table but before I could sit down he added, "I believe you offered me a pint when we met?"

I agreed to get us drinks but was unable to carry all three pints. The pub was crowded and I knew that disaster would result if I tried to carry three full pint glasses; two trips to the bar were required. I brought theirs first and by the time I returned with mine they were laughing and talking like old friends.

"Hugh has offered to let us spend tomorrow on his boat while he visits his mum."

"A day on the boat will discourage you from buying one more effectively than any advice I can give. I think you will agree it is preferable to have a friend with a boat rather than burdening yourself with one. Meet me there at noon. We will get sorted and then I'll pop off."

Which is how it came about that Sam and I spent the next afternoon on board, drinking tea and making dreams of living very different lives. The boat itself was charming but it was rather like being in a fishbowl. Passers-by on the path gawked at us and shouted questions as if we were part of some narrow boat educational display.

"Maybe next time Hugh will let us do this in the evening when there are fewer people around," I suggested.

"Let's close our eyes and shut them out. Forget them. It was so sweet of him to let us do this. I intend to enjoy it."

Inside the boat's railings were built-in benches so we moved to the side with our backs to the path and shut our eyes.

"Now, they are gone; it is only you and I," she said, taking my hand. With eyes closed the drifting water floated me away with Sam and I did not wish to return.

The sun settled behind rain clouds, the wind picked up and before long the cold could not be ignored.

The change in the weather for some reason woke my appetite. "How about it? Are you hungry?"

"Ravenous!"

Over curry dishes and nan at a restaurant around the corner we talked over our day and were in agreement, Hugh was mistaken about narrow boats. The problem wasn't the boat itself, it was the boat's location that was an issue and that could easily be changed: untie it and take it elsewhere. Don't like Little Venice because people on the towpath bother you with questions? Take your floating home to Goring or Birmingham. Tired of the cities? Take it to the country. We were not ready to give up so soon on our dream of becoming river vagabonds.

On our walk home I told Sam of my experience when I thought someone rushed me at the front door.

"You mean someone attempted to attack you?"

"Not sure. It was weird, as if I had a sixth sense that I was followed home. Part of me believed it however unlikely it might be, but part of me argued that I was being foolish and should ignore that fear. Then when I thought I caught a glimpse of someone outside my door the feeling came over me again."

"And then, what? You heard them run up behind you at the front door?"

"It was more like I felt them run at me. It was like wind and there was a sound but not like footsteps."

"Creepy!"

"I know!"

Sam gave me a wry smile, "how long have you been having these episodes? I am sure we can arrange for trained health care professionals to help you."

"You don't believe me?"

"I do want to believe you, but no, I don't believe a ghost was chasing you."

"I didn't say it was a ghost, it might have been a person. I don't know what it was. I do know that something was right behind me when I went in the door. And it was up to no good."

"Well, If you say it is so I believe you. You know what I think? I think you need someone to stay with you tonight and keep you warm and safe." She leaned over and kissed me.

"I feel warmer already."

"Not safer?" she whispered.

"Why are you whispering?"

"Because I am quite sexy," she laughed through her nose and ran down the sidewalk ahead of me, "and that is what we sexy people do, we whisper."

I caught up with her and held her tight, "then do it again." I held her face in my hands and kissed her.

"Remind me later."

But we were too busy later.

Chapter Eight

There is always a sweaty one, she thought, looking at the group assembled before her on exercise bikes. Of course everyone in her "Pump It Up" class perspired; they paid her good money to make them work and would have felt shortchanged if they didn't sweat. But there was always one person drenched in it. Usually a guy. Dripping. On the floor, on the bike and on her if she wasn't careful.

Most of the people who participated in "Pump It Up" were in good shape, healthy and vital. She enjoyed looking at them, admiring their toned physiques as she walked through the group encouraging them. And then she would see the sweaty person and have to look away and return to her bike at the front of the class.

"Up on your pedals!" she yelled over the blasting music. Most had their eyes down as they struggled to maintain the pace she set for them. Some closed their eyes, looking inward to find the will to keep up. And always one or two, sometimes men, sometimes women, met her eyes as if to challenge her. "More!" they seemed to say. "I can do more."

This was when she would change the music to an even faster beat and tell them to increase their bike's resistance by two stops. She watched as some immediately gave up, went down on their seats and backed off the resistance. The next group to go down was the eyes-down group, followed by the inner-lookers leaving only the one or two who challenged her. After a few minutes, near exhaustion yet seeing no evidence of strain or fatigue in her, they too gave up.

This brought the class to an end. She encouraged the group to continue for a few minutes at a comfortable pace to cool down before showering, but she was done. Gathering her things she left as quickly as possible. She'd learned that if she didn't leave the questions would begin. She hated questions.

Chapter Nine

I remember going with Sam to my pub one Saturday night. We had taken the morning train to Henley to watch rowing teams prepare for the Regatta. On the train ride back she had tried to convince me that we should go to the Serpentine at Hyde Park the next day where we could rent a row boat and practice like the Henley rowers. I knew that if we rented a boat she would row a few strokes, get bored with it and ask me to row her around while she trailed her fingers in the water and waved to the other boaters. All she would need was a floppy hat and a parasol.

I suggested that we go to a cinema instead. We agreed to let the weather decide for us and I was surprised how easily she agreed. The sun would take us boating, clouds would send us to the movies. We had dinner on the corner a block from the Crown and stopped in there for a pint afterwards. I had wanted for some time to introduce Will to her. When we took a seat at the bar he was talking to the regular in the brown sweater, with his back to us. Both men laughed loudly, sharing a joke. Will turned back to the bar and noticed us. I promptly introduced him to Sam.

"Oh, I feel like I should know you. Have we met before?" she said.

"I don't believe I've had the pleasure," he replied, reaching across the bar to shake her hand.

"Sorry, you looked familiar," she said sincerely, "but I think I know everyone, don't I? What is it like to manage a pub? Do you ever get up during the night and say, 'I think I'll pop downstairs and have a pint'? Ooh, or a shot of anything I want! I couldn't do it. I couldn't manage a pub. I need the routine of office work to keep me settled. I would go off the rails if we exchanged jobs." A thought crossed her face, "Although...perhaps for a day..."

Will laughed. "You are a gem."

He left us to attend other customers.

Sam leaned against me and nuzzled my neck. Her lips worked their way up to my ear. She whispered into it, "I believe I have seen him before but let's forget him tonight. We are going boating tomorrow!"

"If it is sunny..."

"Silly man, it is always sunny if we want it to be."

***

Fate is cruel. She gives or takes. Some people skate through life doing nothing right and Fate rewards them with riches, happiness and long life. Others never stand a chance. No matter what they do, they can't win. Fate holds them down.   She rubs their noses in the dirt and kicks them in the backside whatever they try.

Most of us win some and lose some and Fate is fine with that.   We don't seem to be a target of either Her bounty or Her maliciousness. We have to make it on our own but at least She doesn't have it in for us.   Maybe She simply doesn't care about us or maybe the ones She targets require all of Her attention.

However, She has two very special categories reserved for a select few.   To these Fate gives and takes.   One group is born with nothing, unattractive, without talent or character.   To them She gives success, wealth and pleasure. As part of the package She throws in greed and selfishness for good measure.   It is for the second group however where Her bi-polar disorder reveals itself.   For this final group She reserves Her deepest love and most severe contempt. To these individuals She gives beauty, charm, intelligence and talent without limit but resolves that their lives will be filled with misery and heartache. She teases them with the prospect of good fortune but dangles it out of reach and ultimates snatches it away.

Little wonder then at the anguish Kat felt. Fate had selected her for the latter category. Practically from birth she stood out from the crowd yet disappointment and misfortune surrounded her. All she wanted to do was disappear from sight, hole up where no one and nothing could inflict pain and be left alone.

She was attractive, not with exotic movie star looks but a kind, open, pretty face that drew people to her. She wore no makeup, simple clothing and kept to herself but could not escape attention. By the time she was twenty she had grown her brown hair long to shield her face from view but the strategy backfired and made her even more attractive so she cut it short again and then stopped trying to hide.

At first she looked for jobs where she could be solitary, not part of a large office or team, but that effort failed because she was quickly found out and then had nowhere to escape and no one to hide behind. She tried other types of jobs, this and that, but it didn't matter. Always the same result. Eventually people would come to know her and then the questions would begin, always the same questions. Ultimately since she was athletic she decided to work at what she enjoyed and deal with the inevitable questions as best she could, which landed her at a fitness club. Leading her classes gave her control; she could avoid the questions by preventing them. Breathless people couldn't ask questions so she drove them hard, made them gasp for air and then left them, panting to recover their wind.

Chapter Ten

Sam often surprised me. She didn't try to be unconventional, it came naturally. She was pleasantly weird. I seldom knew what to expect from her.

We had spent a lovely Sunday morning taking photographs in Regent's Park before the crowds came: Sam climbing a tree, strutting on a footbridge, pouting alone on a park bench, surprising a rose bush. I had a phone full of pictures of her shenanigans. We walked back along the tow path to my place for an afternoon of relaxation. I was in the kitchen making tea when I heard her sobbing in the chair by the window.

"Sam, what's wrong?"

Tears ran down her face. She held her phone for me to watch a video of a battered dog rescued from an abusive owner. She couldn't stop sobbing. I kneeled beside her, holding her hand, "It will be all right, the dog is safe now."

"How could anyone...?"

"I don't know. There are more turds on this earth than I care to think about but one thing makes me optimistic."

"What?"

"Knowing that there are people like you with doggy bags who pick them up."

She looked at me like she couldn't believe I would say something so utterly stupid, then smiling through her tears she shook her head. "I should start with you."

I learned soon thereafter that Sam was not only something of a liar, she was also a cry-er. Not the sad, weepy type. The bawling, sobbing type. Infrequent, but wholehearted. She didn't cry easily. It took something grossly mean to do it, like a bloated refugee child photographed by the side of the road. I guess I may be inured to those things, society being what it is. I am disgusted by them but the next moment I have an email to respond to or coffee to drink and I put them out of mind. She was different. They touched a nerve. When one set her off it reminded me how callous I've become, deadened to deep sympathy.

After the cries she regained her joy but didn't forget.

***

Her roommate was a pig. A slovenly, stupid pig. Kat had found the room on an internet roommate search site. Provide the area in London in which you wish to live, your price range and gender preference and Bob's your uncle, onscreen you have a list of properties with a short write-up of each. Of course you can't trust the write-up anymore than the ones on dating sites but they help narrow the search.

She had called the number provided and the woman she spoke to, named Edith, said she owned the flat and was looking for a roommate. Two bedrooms, large sitting room and fully-fitted kitchen. The price was good so they agreed on a time for her to view it. When she arrived she thought the sitting room was small, not large, her bedroom had only sufficient room for a single bed and the kitchen was spartan. However, the bed and a dresser were included in the price which was a relief because she owned no furniture. Her cooking needs were simple so the kitchen met her needs. More importantly the flat appeared to be tidy which she later realized probably had more to do with the previous tenant than her new roommate.

The opinion Kat had formed when they met was that Edith was a neat, proper woman about ten years her senior, maybe more. She had a habit of sitting with her hands together, at the level of her neck, and tucking her elbows to her side, something Kat had only seen society women with pursed lips do before. Edith did not converse, she questioned, and those questions centered on ensuring that Kat had a job and could be relied on to pay her rent on time. Dubious that being an athletic trainer was an actual job, she had asked to see the pay stub Kat brought. After that she showed no personal interest in Kat which suited Kat just fine; she took the place.

After moving in with her possessions consisting of two bags of clothes and shoes and a box of personal items — all of which fit neatly in the closet and dresser - she soon learned that Edith wasn't at all tidy. Kat watched her take a glass from the cupboard, fill it with water, sit primly in her chair, take a sip, get up and leave the almost-full glass on the end table. Two days later it hadn't moved. It seemed that every item she touched remained where she last touched it. Shoes, nail files, dishes, it didn't matter. After waiting a week Kat thought she might give Edith a nudge by putting the dishes and water glasses on the kitchen counter, however there they remained.

Kat took refuge in her small room. At the foot of her bed she was able to squeeze in a narrow chair for reading.

"Cozy," she told herself. "I have everything I need. More space would be wasted space. It is quiet here and I am satisfied. What more could I want?"

True, she would have liked a separate entrance so she wouldn't have to navigate Edith's pig sty but what was one to do? The rent was cheap, she was snug and really, wasn't a pig sty fundamentally in the same category as those really sweaty people she trained? If the view is unpleasant one need simply look away.

Chapter Eleven

My living room overlooked the communal garden behind the building. Memories of Sam sitting here with her cup of tea were painfully fresh. Vine covered fences, flowering annuals, rose bushes and shady nooks tempted me to lose myself thinking of her, letting my coffee turn cold and the Sunday paper go unread, when the phone rang.

"Did I wake you?" Ellie's voice sounded sharp.

It was 7:00 am on a Sunday so it was a reasonable question.

"No, but you are certainly up early. I'm always awake at this time of the morning however I took you for a late sleeper."

"Not when my thoughts continually race about. I had trouble sleeping. My mind was full of questions. I have been up for hours trying to answer them. Some things don't sound right."

"You are talking about Sam's murder?"

"Yes, it is all I can think about. I need to talk. Will you meet with me?"

"Of course. When and where?"

"The restaurant next to your pub serves breakfast. Meet me there at 9:00 when they open?"

"I'll see you there."

She hung up without a goodbye. I could be there in ten minutes so I used the intervening two hours to go over things on my mind. I was beginning to understand that Ellie and I were wired differently. I was crushed by Sam's death. I felt unable to function normally. I wanted to shut down every time I thought of her. There was a heaviness that made thinking difficult. I couldn't stop remembering her face, her wit and the energy surge she created when I was with her. I wanted to get my hands on the son of a bitch that did this to her but I had no idea even how to find him.

Ellie, it seemed, was different; not only was she able to think clearly, her confidence that we would find him made me believe it too. I put my faith in her.

She was waiting for me outside the restaurant when I arrived ten minutes early; it wasn't open yet. Ellie was dressed casually but looked anything but relaxed. Although seemingly oblivious to the admiring looks that surrounded her I never got the sense that she didn't want the attention. Rather, I believed that she ex-pected it; it was due her because she deserved it. She was accustomed to attention.

This morning, however, she wore slacks and a light jacket over a sweatshirt. I was sur-prised that she even owned one. I'm not certain I would have recognized her if I ran into her amongst the throngs of people on Oxford Street. It was almost as if she was wearing a disguise.

"Why don't restaurants open earlier here? "I asked while we waited. "In America crowds of people would be pounding on the doors by six."

"Because we are civilized," she smiled. "Sundays are for sleeping late, not for gorging oneself before the sun has risen. Why are Americans in such a rush?" I acknowledged her point but countered that coffee early in the morning was good for the soul, something English shopkeepers should keep in mind. We looked inside to see if they were about to open. There were servers gathered in the back and I could smell coffee brewing so there was still hope for my soul.

"Thank you for coming," she said. "I must seem mad."

I explained my theory that we were wired differently and that I appreciated her willingness to share a functioning brain with me. Then I complimented her sweatshirt.

"It is beastly I know but I wasn't at all certain where the day might take us."

"The day? I thought we were meeting for breakfast."

"Yes, and what we discuss at breakfast will help us plan our day."

A woman whose top revealed a discrete amount of cleavage broke away from the servers at the back and walked to the front door to unlock it. Although we were the only customers waiting she looked past us as if hoping someone, let's say, "more upscale" would appear. They didn't so she opened the door and showed us to a table against the wall at the side of the restaurant. I thought it looked cramped and asked for a better table. The hostess explained that most of the tables were reserved. For some reason I didn't believe her and developed an immediate dislike for her. Ellie accepted her explanation and pointed out that the table was in a quiet spot and we had much to discuss.

Once seated she jumped right in, "You told me something about the scene that bothers me. I can't get it out of my head. Can you describe again the shoes that you saw under the shrub?"

I am not a shoe guy. I don't pay much attention to them in general and my attention at the scene was on Sam but I remembered a few details. "They were red high heels and had two or three straps across the front."

"Do you ever remember seeing Sam wear those shoes?"

I didn't. Sam's taste in shoes ran to practical, sturdy, well-made shoes or boots. She liked bright, bold colors and loved prints when it came to tops, dresses and trousers but her footwear was decidedly un-girly which was the only reason I noticed it.

"That is what bothers me," Ellie said. "She never wore flirty shoes. I know she wasn't wearing those shoes that night. She had on those chunky black shoes that I disliked. I believe the shoes you saw belonged to someone else."

"The killer?"

"Perhaps, or an accomplice."

"Or," I added as I felt my brain engage, "a second victim."

"Precisely." Ellie seemed glad that I was keeping up for a change.

"So Sam was barefoot when her body was dumped and...someone...not Sam, lost or maybe left their shoes near her." The realization that this was more complex than it originally seemed, somehow made it less personal. "It's even possible that Sam was not the principal target!"

"It is. You see the problem? One question leads to many, many more. If Sam alone was involved there is a good chance we might know the killer but if another person was involved and that person was the target, the killer could be anyone."

"And what is up with the shoes? Why was Sam barefoot and why were those shoes left at the scene?"

Ellie shook her head in sympathy. "I can't even guess. But, at least it is a clue, the only one we have to go on.

"I have another question," Ellie raised her eyes from her tea cup, "you said the police found her wallet?"

"Yes, all her credit cards and cash appeared to be undisturbed."

"What about her purse?"

"Her purse?"

"You didn't mention it. When the police found the wallet was it in her purse?"

"No, they found the wallet by itself under a bush. I saw the policewoman hold it high to show the others after she found it. Then she looked inside it and confirmed that the ID was Sam's. There was no purse."

"I am certain that she had a purse with her."

"So, we are missing a purse, we have mystery red shoes and possibly there's another victim."

We ate in silence when our food arrived, both of us trying to put together the few clues we had. They were scanty, not enough for me to do more than make wild guesses. I thought about the people at the dinner, a few of whom continued to seem like viable suspects. Neal, sitting thousands of miles away in Hong Kong, couldn't be ruled out. Hugh had been at the party and lived near the scene where her body was found. They were at the top of the list but others could easily be included.

"Lets try to narrow our focus somewhat," I suggested. "It will help me if we can eliminate some names. You've known all the people who were at the dinner longer than I have. Are there any who seem to you to be unlikely suspects?"

"I believe we can safely remove the twins from the list. They were clubbing with Val and Ilyse. The four can vouch for each other. Vince and James seem unlikely. They rarely interacted with Sam. As Directing Manager of the company Vince constantly travels and is seldom in the office. His job is his life, he only thinks of us as employees, not people. James is a sweet man who takes no interest in the office. He works with the rest of us to get his paycheck otherwise he has no interest in any of us. They may have connections to Sam of which we are unaware however I don't think we should focus on them."

"How about Paul and my pick for least favorite co-worker, Rita?"

"She can be a bit harsh, can't she?"

"Harsh? Sharp-tongued, mean and hostile would better describe her. She and Paul make the perfect pair."

"I disagree; they are quite different. Paul is a contrarian, he prefers to go against the flow whereas Rita is lonely and afraid. She wants to be liked but lacks the social skills for that to happen. They are both social outsiders, aren't they? If either had an issue with Sam they might not handle it well. Let's talk to them tomorrow and try to find out if they had any connections outside of work with Sam. Would you talk with Paul? You could ask him if he noticed Neal's reaction to Hugh and see where it leads. I will do the same with Rita."

"I would like to get in touch with Neal too but it will be his first day in the Hong Kong office tomorrow so he may be hard to reach. Worth a

try though."

"Are you ready to go?" she asked.

"Where?"

"Back to the scene."

Chapter Twelve

One friend is all that is needed if that person is a proper friend. Someone who has shared the worst and helps push away the pain, even brings about a smile perhaps. It is enough.

Her friend had done all those things. She shared the worst day of their lives. A day that changed them forever but forged a link that endured. A link so strong that even after a separation of many years they immediately recognized each other outside the Baker Street Station.

"Oh my god! Is that really you Kat?"

Kat nodded, almost shyly. Afraid to believe that this was her friend, the friend she had not seen since the commotion surrounding the incident died down. The incident that destroyed her family and also caused her friend's family to move away taking her best friend with them. But here she was! She looked so happy and ran to her, taking her in her arms and hugging her tighter and tighter.

"Kat! I knew I would find you. I knew it would happen."

They hugged and talked without pause outside the Tube station, just happy to be to-gether.

"I tried and tried to find you. I swear I thought about you every day Kat. I wanted to be with you. I was certain you could cope without anyone but I knew I could make you smile if I was with you. You are so strong and never need help. I wanted to do whatever I could, but not until I got myself better. I was a total disaster. Ooh, you don't need to hear about that.   I'm good now and seeing you again makes me hap-pier than I've ever been. Come to my flat, we will have a bottle of wine and talk for hours. Do!"

The flat was small but filled with colors like a prism as if items had been selected for their color not their function. Kat who chose grays and beige for her own room felt oddly comfortable. She began to relax, wishing she could be more like the person smiling at her. After pushing away the world for so long, it was difficult to let anyone inside — even her one special friend. Not that she resisted; she simply needed to relearn how to do it. The wine helped. The smiles helped. They sat on the floor across a coffee table from each other.

"I was in bad shape but it was so much worse for you, Kat. How did you manage? When the monster took that girl your life changed so much more than mine did. I needed help and when we moved to a new town I could try to forget about the life I had before and what had happened. Out of sight out of mind you know, but oh god, when I went to bed every night I could not forget about you. It was like I kept you separated in my mind from the bad things. I even talked to you in my head. You won't believe this but one time in an imaginary conversation you told me to be a happy person. To let it all go. You said that you wanted me to do it because I could make others feel good. I know you didn't really say it but it meant so much to me. You made it possible for me to move on. I cannot ever thank you enough because although the conversation wasn't real, that's exactly what you would have said."

She paused, letting a few moments pass before changing the subject.

"Will you tell me what it was like for you after I left? Can you talk about it? Do you even want to?"

"I believe I can but before I do, I want you to know you are right, that is what I would have told you. You are special — you make people happy. Please never stop doing that. It is still difficult for me to talk about what happened. I have tried so hard and for so long not to think about it. I don't know how much I can tell. At first of course there was the shame."

"Shame?   Kat you didn't do anything wrong!"

"I was ashamed that no one believed me. It would have all turned out so differently if they had. I didn't understand. I still don't understand. Why was I ignored? As if I wasn't a person. Others' voices mattered; mine didn't. I felt humiliated."

"No Kat, no, it wasn't you. It was the circumstances. It is only natural for the police to think that a child might lie to protect her father. You told the truth. You couldn't do more than that. Don't forget, they didn't believe me either. If only we could have seen the license number."

"I was a liar. That is what everyone said. I had no worth. Instead they believed that lying cow of a woman. She was as much a monster as the pervert who drove away. She told them what they wanted to hear. Why did she say it was my father's car she saw? She didn't even see the car. Did she do it to get attention? The police and the television people ate it up. My father never had a chance. All the publicity, all the hearings, all the questions... Even now, as soon as I am recognized as "that girl" the questions begin all over again." Kat's voice trailed off. She no longer could cry, there had been too much of that and it didn't change anything. She tried to sip her wine but raising the glass was too hard. Everything felt heavy. She couldn't drink. She was so tired.

Arms encircled her from behind and held tight, rocking her, comforting her. She felt the heaviness subside, replaced by an awareness. Senses and feelings, not thoughts. This moment, being held. Only this moment. No other. She sensed warm breath on the back of her neck followed by the light pressure of a head coming to rest there. A tear fell on her neck followed by sobs even as the rocking continued. She couldn't cry too but she could be held. She could let her in.

"I am so so sorry for you, Kat," between the sobs. Kat turned and put her face against the wet cheek, returning the hug, holding tight to the moment. Slowly the sobs fell away and she clasped her closer. Without thought Kat moved her head slowly to the left, her lips brushing eye- lids, then nose and then touching the lips of her one true friend.

Chapter Thirteen

Not a trace remained. The police had raked, bagged and removed every bit of debris from under the shrubbery. I wondered what Ellie expected to find. If the purse had been here it was now in the custody of the police.

We stood on the bridge overlooking the spot Sam's body had been dumped, exactly where we stood two days before. A block in front of us we could see a narrow boat entering the tunnel under Edgware Road from the opposite side. Above the tunnel traffic on Edgware edged its way slowly but with evident purpose, the sound of traffic strangely muted by trees growing tall on both sides of the canal.

"Why did we come here?" I asked. "You didn't expect to find the purse. We knew the police had thoroughly swept the crime scene so what are we doing here?"

She surveyed the buildings, left and right, then studied the canal boats on one of which a group of people clinked wine glasses and laughed. She stared at them intently.

"I wonder how strange it would be to live in the houses here with the narrow boat community right outside your front door. Imagine, surrounded by these mansions and expensive houses is a transient society that at any time can untie their homes and quietly drift away. It would be like having a gypsy caravan camped in the middle of your street. Unquestionably the boats are quaint and add color and character to the neighborhood but strictly speaking they do not belong. They don't participate in the neighborhood's society. Could two more different lifestyles exist beside each other anywhere else in the world?"

The question sounded rhetorical, Ellie thinking out loud. Living in this area I have seen many people walk along the tow path, admiring the boats on one side and the houses on the other, but I don't remember seeing a single resident come from or go into the houses. I assumed they used rear entrances to avoid the boat owners. Possibly they didn't want to interact with them but were quite willing to include them in their view.

She gave me a questioning look. "Are we looking in the correct direction?" This time she did want an answer but I didn't have one.

"What other direction is there?"

"Perhaps we shouldn't limit our view to the canal."

"You mean we should consider that someone who lives in one of these houses was responsible?"

"Not necessarily one of these houses but someone who lives in the neighborhood. Did Sam know anyone else in the area besides you and Hugh?"

"She never spoke of anyone."

"It does seem a bit posh for Sam's tastes," Ellie admitted. "However I feel certain that in some way this neighborhood is involved." Her eyes widened, "Oh my God! What if the crime scene was staged?"

"Staged?"

"Consider this: why did the murderer go to the effort of bringing her body by boat and carrying it to the Toll house, then leaving it with a wallet containing her ID and someone else's shoes nearby?"

"To hide the body...where else could a person hide it around here?"

"It wasn't hidden! It was near a popular path. Two narrow boats are tied up no more than fifty feet from where she was found. If the killer was trying to hide Sam's body he did a damned poor job of it. She was discovered virtually at first light. It would have been much easier for the killer to put her body in the canal. It would have taken at least as long for it to be found. But he couldn't do that because the current might have taken the body downstream and he didn't want to take that chance because he wanted her to be found here."

"For what reason?"

She looked carefully at me, "One reason might be that he intended to implicate you. You dated her and have a nearby flat."

I let that sink in. Someone had murdered Sam to get at me?

"Wait, no, it wasn't me they were after. I don't have a boat. Remember? The suspect needed to have a boat to put the body where it was. In order for the killer to throw suspicion on someone that person must have a boat to be considered. That rules me out but it leaves..."

"Hugh! Of course!"

"If so, he remains a legitimate suspect on one hand and on the other hand he could be the victim of the killer's efforts to cast suspicion on him. Let's go speak with Hugh."

His boat was a short walk further along the tow path but Hugh wasn't there and neighboring boat owners said they hadn't seen him since Friday.   He had told me he didn't carry a mobile phone so calling him was not an option. It was possible that the police had taken him into custody but we knew they would not tell us about anyone they were investigating.   We needed to try to contact him.

"If they are not holding him he could be with a friend," I said. "I know he started dating a woman recently."

"Let's hope the police have him because if not he could be in danger. Do you know anyone we could call?"

"I have his mother's phone number.   He gave it to me in case anything came up when Sam and I stayed on his boat."

"Call her!"

I needed to have a plan when I called her. An unknown American man calling her out of the blue to ask if her son was in jail might not get far, so I used Sam's approach and lied — just a little. I told her I was a friend of Hugh's who was supposed to meet him at his boat but he wasn't there. "Any idea where he is?"

"I haven't spoken with Hugh for days. You said you are a friend? I am sorry I am unable to help."

"Do you know anyone else who might know? Hugh said he doesn't carry a phone so I was hoping a friend or family member might know where he is."

"I don't know his friends but I am his only remaining family. He is otherwise alone."

"Oh, no ex wives or children?"

"He lives alone now."

That seemed a curious thing to say. I could only assume he was not alone before.

"Is something wrong?" She became worried.

"I am sure he is well. He probably forgot that we were planning to meet." I reassured her that it was no doubt just a mix up. No reason to worry her at this time. I ended the call asking her to have Hugh call me when she heard from him.

It was something of a stretch to claim that I was his friend. Sam and I had visited him twice since the day on his boat: once to share a bottle of wine with him, and once with the woman he was seeing. We met at his boat and the four of us walked together to a restaurant overlooking the canal. I only knew that her first name was Susan. The only other times I had spoken to him were several chance meetings at the Crown after work. I actually hadn't encountered him often and certainly didn't know him well.

I suggested to Ellie that we return to the Crown which should be open by now for lunch and ask Will, who seemed to know Hugh better than I did.

The Crown was busier than I expected for a Sunday morning but Will was in his usual place behind the bar. His smile brightened when he saw Ellie with me.

"A pleasure to see you two! What can I get for you?"

"It might be a bit too early for a drink but I do have a question I'd like to ask," I said.

"Two Bloody Marys it is!" He began pour-
ing the ingredients.

"I stand corrected, it is a perfect time of
day for a drink," I laughed. "So, my question is:
do you happen to know Hugh's surname?"

Will turned his back for a moment to
reach for a spoon to mix the drinks. When he
finished stirring and brought us the drinks I
thought his smile had dimmed. "Sorry, I don't."
He placed the drinks in front of us and started
to move away.

"Do you know someone who might know?"
Ellie asked, touching his arm.

Whether it was her touch or the note of
urgency in her voice, Will stopped.

"Is something wrong?"

"We don't know," she replied. "He wasn't
at his boat and his neighbors haven't seen him
recently. Please, we simply want to contact
him."

Will looked nervously around to be certain
no one would hear. "I shouldn't tell you this.
Right? He is a private sort of chap. Doesn't like

being talked about. Stephen would be your man. He may not tell you anything but he would know."

Stephen, the man who struggled to stay upright? I couldn't imagine how he and Hugh were in any way connected.

"Thank you, Will. Sincerely thank you," she said earnestly, showing she understood that he was risking Hugh's displeasure.

"Right. I'll be going upstairs to help with the food as soon as Thomas comes in. It is mad up there. No one seems to want to cook at home on a Sunday." He wiped his hands on a bar towel. "Good luck."

Although he didn't leave for another five minutes, it was clear that Will wanted to be done with the conversation. When Thomas made his appearance behind the bar to relieve Will, we recognized him as the Australian server who had caught Ilyse's eye at the farewell dinner. He didn't recognize me but came right up to Ellie.

"You alright? Like another?" he gestured to her drink. She declined but I asked for one, if for no other reason than get the opportunity to talk with him. When he brought the drink I asked if he had seen Hugh recently.

"The bloke with the boat? Haven't seen him since your dinner party. Terribly sad about your friend. Nasty business. Made me sick when the police spoke to me about it."

"How about Stephen? Has he been in to-day?"

"Not yet. He won't tumble in until past five."

"Thank you," Ellie rewarded him with a smile. I don't believe he would have moved from the spot in front of her if the man next to me hadn't ordered a pint.

"Shall we wait for Stephen?"

Before she could answer Thomas was back. "Almost forgot. I put your friend's purse in the back. Appears she forgot it after the dinner. Would you like to take it to her family?"

"What a good idea, yes, please." I was impressed with how well Ellie disguised her sur-prise at hearing that the purse was here. She smiled again causing him to hurry to the back. Her smile turned to a questioning look when he left. "How could she forget her purse?" she asked. Minutes passed, when he returned from the back room he looked as confused as we felt.

"Be right back," he said leaving us to run upstairs to the dining area. Returning almost immediately, he shook his head. "Will ain't seen it either. Odd. I know I put it there."

"Perhaps the police took the purse as evidence?"

Thomas gave Ellie a guilty look. "You see, I may not have mentioned it to them. Don't like talking with the police. My mind goes blank and I can't remember anything. Makes me jittery. Totally forgot about it until I saw you this minute. Do they know who did it?"

I answered, "Not yet. There are a number of suspects. We are trying to help the police." (It was another small lie, I thought.) "Do you remember anything out of the ordinary at the dinner?"

His head shook in denial while he tried to remember. "Nothing. Only the purse. It was under her chair when everyone left. I know it was her chair because she was the first person I noticed in the room. She was like fireworks. It was a pleasure to be near her. When I found it I knew right off it was her purse. Under her chair and had rainbows on it. Colorful. Seemed to match her. Immediately I put it in the office thinking she'd come back for it. Then I left for the night. Never thought about it again until now."

"Did you notice, was her wallet in it?"

"I didn't look inside. Never look in a woman's purse, I learned that from my sisters. It felt heavy but I don't know."

"Does anyone other than you or Will go into the office?"

"All the pub staff uses the office to hang their coats. Tradesmen leave their invoices there. Some of the regular customers go in to use their phones when the pub is noisy. It is not what you might call 'secure.' I suppose I should have put it somewhere else but honestly I expected her to come back for it. I am an idiot. I am sorry." His head hung.

"You did what you thought was best at the time," Ellie reassured him. "Perhaps someone moved it to a safer place. It may turn up."

"I only saw her that one night, but I remember her so well. Wish I could have known her better. She seemed like fun."

I certainly knew how he felt; Sam had that effect on me, too. With her dark hair cut short, straight out of the 1930s, ringlets and all, and a mouth like a small animal, playful and naughty. It moved left, right, grimaced, smiled and pouted — as independent as she was. I learned I couldn't trust that mouth, not only because of the lies it told but also because of the lies it showed.

Smiles, grimaces and pouts didn't necessarily indicate her feelings at all. They were players using her face as a stage but disconnected from feelings. They were part of the fun. Doing their own thing. Set free like that they mesmerized me. As did she, even as a memory. A memory that refused to fade. Time did not heal, no matter what people claimed.

"If the purse turns up please be sure to tell me," I asked, feeling the pain renew.

Chapter Fourteen

Is it OK to laugh when a person falls flat on top of a drunk? What if they fall when trying to dance and the person is laughing so hard she can't get up? Should you help? This was our dilemma when the team of Ilyse and Valerie came to our aid at the Crown. We thought with their help Stephen might tell us how to locate Hugh. Ellie and I had been unsuccessful in getting him to talk. We hoped that Stephen remembered them flirting with him two nights previous. We weren't terribly optimistic that he remembered anything or that we could understand what he said but it was worth a try. Apparently the two pretty young women had made a lasting impression.

"Tum! Redam sal yonny oon sommat," he said excitedly in greeting as he slid over in the booth to make room for them. Ellie and I were across the table as French, German and what-ever Stephen was speaking flowed heartily be-tween the three. Ilyse put her arm around his shoulder and squeezed laughter from him like a squeaky toy.

I tried interjecting, "Stephen, can you tell us where Hugh is?" He ignored me and began to wiggle like he wanted to get up. The two women moved from the booth. He slid out, took Val by the hand and began to dance something that looked like a pantomime combination of the jitterbug and the tango. Val went along with it until he was about to dip her when she pulled Ilyse into the action — for stability I suspect. In the background someone put on some music which made it at least seem like they were dancing. Ilyse, always the physical one, took Stephen in her arms and push-pulled him around the floor until he attempted to spin her which re-sulted with them on the floor, her on top of him, laughing, and a round of applause from the pub's patrons. Thomas, the Australian, got mixed up in the melee trying to free Ilyse from Stephen's clutch which led to more laughter and confusion. Eventually Val and Ellie were able to distract Stephen. I lifted him to his feet while Thomas and Ilyse helped each other up. After Stephen was settled back in his booth Val took over. She told us to leave the two of them. She would "manage this debacle."

As I watched from the bar she spoke to him very slowly. He began to wiggle again but she had him cornered in the booth. She moved her index finger in front of his face like the pen-dulum of a clock. All I could hear was her voice saying firmly "Non, non, non" to the beat of her finger. When the movement stopped she began tapping him on the chest. At first he grinned at her but the longer the tapping continued the more serious his face became. When she stopped tapping he began talking.

116

"Can she understand him?" asked Thomas.

"Can he understand her?" I replied.

She shook her head at him again, apparently dissatisfied with an answer, and raised her finger but before the tapping resumed he must have told her what she wanted because instead of a tap he got two kisses, one on each cheek. The interrogation over and rewarded with kisses he smiled the rest of the evening.

Val joined us at the bar.

"Well?" I asked when she didn't say anything.

"As you said, it is well. I explained him, 'you must not speak me those funny words. It is no good. To me only English words.' Then he spoke me well. English words. Some nights he stay on the boat of Hugh. Perhaps sick perhaps drink too much but Hugh help him. This week Hugh not here. He stay with girlfriend, Suzanne."

"Was it Susan maybe? I met a woman named Susan with him."

"It is what I said."

For Val, there was never any uncertainty. She would never say she might do this or that. She either would do it or she would not do it. Subject closed. And she was never mistaken.

Ellie shot me a warning look. There was no room for disagreement with Val so I chose a different route, "That is wonderful information, thank you Val." I could see that she liked the compliment. It was deserved; after all she had successfully communicated with Stephen when no one else could. "Did he tell you anything more?"

"That is all."

"How do you do it, Val?" Ilyse added. "I fell on the floor trying to get him to talk and failed. Then you swooped in and settled the matter."

"It is a small thing, telling a man. They are like the children, be nice but certain." She looked over to Stephen in his booth and winked. He returned it with a gentlemanly nod.

Knowing that Hugh was not in police custody and seemingly safe was reassuring but didn't answer any of our questions. Ellie brought

Val and Ilyse up to speed and asked Thomas to tell them about Sam's missing purse. He had moved closely beside Ilyse after freeing her from the clutches of Stephen. He related how he found the purse then left it in the office and how we discovered earlier that it was missing. He suggested to Ilyse if she'd give him her number he'd text her when anything turned up.

I knew he had other reasons to ask for her number and under different circumstances I would not have thought it unusual for him to ask but Thomas had been present at the dinner, he'd admitted to being attracted to Sam, and, really did his story about the purse hold together? Couldn't he have contrived the story? Or, let's say that she did forget her purse, what if she returned for it after everyone had left and things went south from there? We had more questions now and more people to suspect than earlier in the day when Ellie and I met for breakfast.

When the four of us left the Crown I hinted to Ilyse that she should hold off going out with Thomas for now. She quickly cut me short saying she too thought his story about the missing purse raised questions. "However, if he's the killer why did he even mention the purse? Why would he call attention to himself?" she said, adding "I want to believe him but only in part because he is so darn cute."

Val, in a rare attempt at humor added, "do not worry, I can have for you the number of Stephen, if you wish a lover."

***

After Val and Elyse parted with us, Ellie and I walked on in silence.

I broke the silence a block later, "Does it seem odd that Val was able to get Stephen to speak intelligible English? I wonder if the singing and gibberish is an act."

"I was thinking the same thing. Perhaps we should try to find out more about him."

"Ellie, it seems that all we do is uncover additional suspects. The whole thing is becoming so complex. We have clues that don't lead anywhere, plenty of suspects to consider, but none that seem likely. It's overwhelming. I'm beginning to wonder if we are in over our heads,"

I was feeling helpless. We had made some progress, yet the plain truth was that we had no idea who was involved and, worse, we had no direction to proceed.

"Perhaps we are. But what choice do we have? Are you suggesting we should give up? Could you sleep at night if we did? Seriously, could you actually say to yourself, 'oh well, I tried. Hope they get Sam's killer' and just walk away?"

"Of course not, I..."

"Because I can't do that. I will not let Sam become a cold case. If the police solve it, fine, but until they do I will not give up on her."

"OK, you're right. Totally. I'm frustrated and angry."

I told her about my father being shot and the sense of helplessness I felt then.

"It's worse this time. Sam is gone! I want to get this bastard, and it is making me nuts that we're not making any real progress. It's like the same thing happening all over."

"This time is different though, isn't it? This time you are doing something, not waiting around. That makes all the difference. We'll find out who did it. I know we will."

We had walked past the Toll House, crossed the bridge and turned onto Bishop's Bridge Road. I wasn't aware of our intended destination and let Ellie lead the way.

"You know, Ellie, I try to be reasonable and easy-going. Usually, I'm able to control my emotions regardless of what happens. There's a limit to that, however. I have a breaking point and when I reach it I lose all compassion. I simply want revenge. When I think about Sam's killer, he has already gone beyond that point, beyond where I have any forgiveness. I hope the police catch him, Ellie, because honestly I don't know what I would do if I were to get to him first. I'm afraid I would want to even the score."

"I get it. I understand your anger and frustration. It's perfectly natural, but the only thing that really matters is catching this man."

We had to make way on the sidewalk for a woman walking four dogs on leash. She seemed barely in control as they pulled her from side to side.

"Always loved dogs," I said, mostly to myself. We reached a crosswalk and waited for the light. "What is driving you, Ellie? I understand that you were close to Sam too, but why are you so determined? Why is it so important to you that we find the killer? What haven't you told me?"

Ellie looked away for a moment. When she turned back I thought she was about to cry. Instead, she ignored my questions and changed the subject.

"We have suspects and clues but do you know what we desperately need?" She stopped walking and waited for my answer. When I offered nothing she answered her own question. "A motive. We have no goddamn idea why anyone would kill Sam. Without that, the clues don't add up, we have no insight to the suspects and, you are right, we are floundering. Directionless; we have nowhere to focus."

We resumed walking. She asked, "Did Sam ever mention to you a serious incident from her past?"

"An incident?"

"One night Sam was depressed. When I asked her why, she said it was the anniversary of an event that occurred when she was young. Of course I asked her to tell me about it but she refused. I had never seen her so solemn. I think whatever happened long ago may be related to her murder. It still disturbed her. If we knew what occurred it could lead us to the motive for her murder."

We had turned left on Queensway, heading I guessed for Kensington Gardens. It was late to be going to the park but at this time of year hundreds of flowers were blooming at their peak and were as good an excuse as any to spend time in the park. Talking on a park bench suited me.

"So she never mentioned it to you?"

"She seldom spoke of her past," I admitted "and I didn't press her to tell me. I don't know where she grew up or what her parents were like or even if they are alive. She never once mentioned them." We were nearing the park. Ellie slowed again. I tried to remember if Sam had referenced anything from her past.

"She lived very much in the present," I added. "From time to time she told me about guys she had dated but they seemed recent and no big deal. Once when we were in Coventry Gardens she saw someone she thought she knew. It turned out to be a stranger but Sam said the person reminded her of a friend who moved away when she was young. She'd been looking for the friend for years. That is the only thing I can think of."

"Not much to go on is it? Would you like to come in? This is where I live. My flat is small but I have access to the private garden square. We can talk there."

We walked through the building to the garden which was entirely enclosed by the block of apartment buildings. An older woman on a park bench sprinkled seeds for small birds on the path before her. The birds waited patiently until she tossed the seeds with the sweep of her hand then they hopped about, eating as quickly as possible.

Ellie nodded to her as we strolled to a bench under a chestnut tree breaking into leaf. "She does this every evening. The birds wait for her and land at her feet when she arrives."

"This is very peaceful."

"I took the flat because of the gardens. It might seem silly because the gardens in Kensington are only a block away. I enjoy watching people there especially when the sun is shining and everyone who comes to the park is feeling happy but it becomes so crowded. When it does it is pleasant to sit here alone and enjoy the quiet."

It was quiet. I could hear the birds pecking at the seed on the path.

Ellie seemed content to say no more. I guessed that she too was trying to decide what our next move should be. On my way home I could walk by Hugh's boat and leave a note for him to call me. It would be a feeble effort but it was something and our options were limited. I wanted to know more about the childhood incident that had disturbed Sam. It was unlike her to guard her privacy. She was open, in fact brazen, about sharing personal info.

She had been so lively and cheerful it was difficult to imagine troubles when she was young. She told me she didn't have time to think about the past. Now I had learned there was something in her past she apparently didn't want to talk about, almost as if she was ashamed by it.

"When you suggested that Sam was killed because of something in her past, I don't know why but I doubted you, Ellie. Now the more I think it over the more I am inclined to agree with you. Sam did not have secrets. That wasn't her way. She delighted in putting it out there for the world to see. So if there was something she wouldn't talk about, it must be significant."

"I'm sorry. I didn't answer your question earlier. You asked why I am determined to find Sam's killer. I needed first to tell you about the night Sam mentioned her past to me. It shocked me to see her depressed. It was an entirely different side of Sam. She didn't simply refuse to give me details about it, she was defiant, as if protective of that memory. It was my first glimpse of vulnerability in Sam, the first time I saw her as a more complex human being. This memory mattered deeply to her. I always loved her joy and her energy and they were a huge part of her but this was something more, something fundamental. Something she guarded. I cannot think of Sam without remembering her that night. That is what remains for me. To think that someone took her..."

Ellie looked away. The woman who had been feeding birds gathered her purse, an umbrella and the seed bag. She stood to leave. Meal time was finished. The birds scattered, except for one which looked up at the woman and waited. The woman smiled, took a small handful of seed and held her hand out. The bird flitted to her hand, cocked its head to the side and eyed the woman for a moment before eating the seed. When the seed was gone it flew to a tangle of bushes and disappeared. The woman looked in its direction, sighed then limped heavily down the path to her building.

Twilight transitioned into night. Silence surrounded us. Two lamp posts, one at each end of the garden provided dim lighting for the area.

It was time for me to go. Standing I said, "Thank you, Ellie. I believe you would do this without me but I couldn't do it without you."

She looked at me, "I am sorry. I've not been very good company, have I? We must keep trying. Thank you for helping."

"See you tomorrow, OK? Try to get some sleep. A new day, I'm sure we'll make more progress."

She smiled weakly. "I hope you are correct."

"Are you alright? Would you like me stay on a little longer?"

"I think I will sit here and enjoy the quiet, thank you."

I smiled and waved good night. Before leaving the garden I looked back at her. She stared absently into the bushes where the bird had disappeared.

Chapter Fifteen

Even the sweaty guys didn't bother her now. Disgusting though they were she could tolerate them now that her life had changed. That did not mean that she went easier on the people in her classes. If anything, she had more energy, drove them harder and was slow to recognize when they did not keep pace. No one challenged her. No one dared to make eye contact. They were surprised when she lingered after class. Usually she was gone before they dismounted. However they were somewhat afraid of her, intimidated after so many classes by her intensity, and therefore were too cautious to begin a conversation with her. And probably most importantly, they were exhausted.

"I have someone," she told herself as she watched the class leave for the showers. Her face grinned back at her in the mirrors lining the exercise room. With the room to herself she decreased the volume of the exercise music, overcoming the urge to dance by tapping her hand to the beat. A guilty smile returned. She tried to suppress it and couldn't. "I have some-one." This feeling would require time for her to adjust to.

***

I tried to call Neal first thing the next morning. With the seven hour time difference I hoped to catch him at the end of his work day. In a meeting, his assistant said. He would call me back.

Paul was easier to speak to; he was in his office with his back to me. I knocked on his open door and walked in.

"Hello! What's on your mind?" he asked, turning to face me.

I seldom seemed to be in synch with Paul. In the past every one of our discussions had become awkward at some point. This one was likely to be the worst. I tried to be upbeat but direct, "I have a call into Neal. Ellie is talking to Rita. We want to talk to everyone about the night Sam died."

"Still playing detectives, eh? I feel terrible about her. I liked Sam. You may have noticed that I don't care for many people."

I nodded.

"High standards. That's the reason. At least that is what I tell myself. Truth is I am un-comfortable around people. Don't misunder-stand, I won't tolerate fools, and there are so many of them. There are very few people I want to be with. Yet I'm not comfortable even with the ones I like. What I liked about Sam was that she knew when to leave. She let me be. She made me comfortable."

I told him about Val noticing an odd reaction from Neal when Sam introduced Hugh. I wondered had he also seen it?

"I do remember that. He seemed frustrated with her, as if he was saying 'what the hell?' I never liked Neal. Wasn't sorry to see him go to China. The farther the better. He will be able to drive his Asian cars to his heart's content. If you live in England you should drive an English automobile. Simple as that. Or at least a European one."

"Val thought Neal acted jealous."

"Jealous? That doesn't make sense. His flight was going to depart eight hours later the next morning. He was leaving everyone behind. Including Sam. Why would he be jealous? He was about to lead a new life fifteen thousand miles away. No, I think Sam had done something Neal didn't like. He had always looked out for her, you know? Hired her, volunteered to mentor her and even recommended her for promotions."

"Does that seem suspicious to you? He isn't the kind of guy to go out of his way to help others. He is so self-promoting. Why would he help Sam? Maybe they were having a relation-ship?"

"Perhaps, you never know. I rather feel that he was keeping an eye out for her, like an older brother. I doubt that Neal is your man. If you want my opinion as to whom you should suspect it would be that fellow with a boat. Neal seemed not to like him. Another one was that Australian at the pub."

"Thomas? Why him?"

"Two reasons. First: he couldn't take his eyes off Sam. Second: his ring tone. Did you hear it when he got a call? Big band music! Who in their right mind listens to that? Nails on the chalk board when I hear it. Cannot stand it. Wouldn't trust anyone who listens to it, certainly no one who chooses it for their ring tone. My god!"

Before he launched into another tirade I left Paul shaking his head. I tended to agree with him that a romance between Sam and Neal was unlikely. They were ill-matched in every way and when would she have had time? Two affairs at the same time with me and her woman lover would have been hard enough to manage. A third affair seemed beyond difficult. Paul himself was an improbable suspect. He could have easily thrown suspicion on Neal but he actually defended him despite not liking him personally. And who did he suspect? A man because he liked big band music! His reason for pointing out Hugh at least made sense but, no, I didn't think Paul was our guy.

While waiting for Neal to return my call I tried to hack into Sam's social media accounts. She seldom posted but maybe a message would give us a clue or a friend who would stand out. I was able to guess that Sam's password of choice was "password" but as I expected there was very little activity in any of her accounts. Internet search engines revealed nothing new about her either. For a woman with her big personality she had little on-line presence.

About the time I thought it was too late in Hong Kong for Neal to call, he called.

"Sorry. Sales meetings, staff to be introduced to, customer dinner, blah, blah blah. You know, the busy life of an international executive. How are you?"

"Not well. Have you heard about Samantha?"

"The moment I stepped off the airplane here police were waiting to question me. Understandable. It doesn't look good when a person leaves the country hours after having dinner with the victim of a homicide. Have they found the person who did it?"

I told him that an hour ago Ellie had called the detective handling the case for an update. They were "following up on a number of leads" he said which meant to us that they had no good leads. Ellie and I were trying to help in our own way.

"Good luck. I mean that. I want the person caught. Samantha was special."

"We have spoken to everyone who was at your dinner, even the servers. We have some ideas but, like the police, nothing solid. When we talked to Valerie she said she noticed that you had an odd reaction when Samantha introduced Hugh to you."

There was a lengthy pause.

"Are you still on the line Neal?"

"I am."

"Well? What was going on?"

"I doubt that it has anything to do with what happened to Samantha."

"But if it does?"

"Yes, I know. I did mention it to the police here for that reason. The matter is sensitive. I need your word that you and Ellie won't tell anyone. I want people to remember Samantha the way she was."

"You have my word. I swear."

"Believe me I will hold you to that even from the other side of the world." There was another long pause. "I grew up across the street from a young girl — perhaps four or five years younger than me. She and a friend named Kat witnessed the abduction of a classmate. The girl who was taken was found dead the next morning."

"Oh god, Sam saw the abduction?"

"Unfortunately it gets worse. One of the teachers said she saw it happen and identified Kat's father as the man who took the child."

"Was he convicted?"

"Not by the police. Kat said she saw a different man, not her father, put the girl in a car trunk and drive away. Samantha backed her up. They both said they were near enough to see the man's face clearly and that it was not Kat's father. The police were inclined to doubt the girls' story but events settled the matter before the police acted. The murder of a young school girl sells newspapers so the daily papers went after the father with a thousand knives. Photos of him were front page news. Editorials called for him to be immediately jailed. Kat was caught up in it because she publicly defended him which sold more newspapers and kept her in the public eye. Samantha faired better and because she was a minor her name was withheld from the press."

"That's the reason nothing came up on the internet when I searched her? Her name was not released?"

"Yes, and it was fortunate because it soon became a free-for-all. Kat's mother suddenly left. Moved to France, leaving daughter and accused husband behind. Possibly because she knew he was guilty but it could have been simply to escape the public scrutiny. The daily papers said her departure was proof that he had done it. Then a few days later he was found drowned. Justice! At least according to the media. As a result of all this Samantha had some issues. Her family moved away to protect her from the media circus and let her recover. Our families stayed in touch."

"That's why you got Sam the job?"

"Sure, I tried to help her."

"Why did you react to Hugh the way you did?"

"I coached Samantha at work. She was doing great. I wanted her to be successful at her job and I also wanted her to have a good life. Put that whole, awful incident behind her. Move on I told her. She did until she met your friend Hugh whose wife and daughter were killed, you know."

"His mother alluded to that when I spoke to her. Did Sam say how they died?"

"That was the issue. He told Samantha that a driver under the influence hit and killed them. It was some years past. Samantha identified with the rage he still feels. When she told me about it I recommended she stay away from him. No good could come from stirring up those feelings. So when he showed up at the dinner of course I was not pleased to see him."

"Any idea if he knew about her past?"

"I think she only told him that she had lost someone too and sympathized for his loss. I don't believe that she told him what had happened. I had advised her over and over not to talk about it, certainly not to strangers. I truly hope she listened to me…"

He put his hand over the phone, apparently to say something to a person he was with.

"I have to go. Mention Kat's name to Ellie; she will remember the case. Find the person who did this, please. Call me if you need anything. Do you understand me? Anything."

I promised to keep him in the loop when I ended the call. While I didn't entirely buy the explanation of his reaction to Hugh it was plausible; the story about Sam would be easy enough to confirm. Harder, far harder, for me to accept that I knew so little about her past. For two months I had been closer to Sam than I'd ever been with anyone. I had loved being with her, telling her my plans, laughing at her criticisms of the conventional habits of people we knew and sharing her joy of being different. In other words I loved knowing her. Knowing her? I knew so little about her. I wondered, how long does it take to really know someone?

Chapter Sixteen

Someone else? It gave her chills to think there was someone else. Fighting back nausea she tried to think clearly. Of course Sam would be dating someone when they finally reconnected. Everyone loved her. They should love her. It wasn't as if she expected Sam to have hidden away for years in a darkened room hoping someday to bump into her. No, it wasn't her fault. No blame, but that didn't take away the fear and pain which continued to build. What now? What now?

Sam was sitting on the floor at Kat's feet, head turned, ashamed to meet her eyes. "I had to tell you. I had to be honest. I wanted to tell you about him that first night when we finally saw each other again but I couldn't do it then. Being with you again was so wonderful. I mean, things happened so quickly and before I knew it I had waited too long. Oh Kat, please don't be hurt. You are the last person I would ever want to hurt. Hate me...hit me...kick me...but don't hurt. What can I do? Please tell me. I will do any-thing."

Sam looked smaller, her shoulders shrunken, head bowed, the lovely face filled with the pain Kat too was feeling. Kat slid from her chair and kneeled before Sam. "What now? What do we do?" She put her hand on Sam's face, gently pulling it to her shoulder, whispering "I love you."

A thousand times she whispered it.

***

When I told her about my conversation with Neal, Ellie jumped from her chair, "Oh my god, of course I remember about Kat. The story was all over the news. Sam was the other girl? I never dreamed. Holy shit! Holy fucking shit!"

She dialed the phone. "Rita, come to my office immediately! As fast as you can. Hurry, it is urgent. Just do it!"

Rita worked one floor above us. Apparently she ran down the stairs; she was in Ellie's office moments later. "I do NOT appreciate being ordered about like a common..."

Ellie cut her off, "sorry, yes I know. I will explain later. What I need you to do is critically important. You were the first person I thought of."

With her hands on her hips after being interrupted, Rita was confused. She had raced downstairs to give Ellie a piece of her mind. How dare Ellie order her like that! And now to be cut off before she got properly worked up. Instinctively she wanted to walk straight out of that office. That's what confused her. She didn't walk out, she stayed. Ellie was one of the few people in the company that she trusted. Direct, understanding and sincere, Ellie had always treated her with respect, unlike some people. Anyone other than Ellie would have received an earful. Cautiously but tersely Rita ventured, "What is it?" Not that she was agreeing to anything.

"We need you to locate Kat for us."

Rita did not respond.

"You do remember Kat don't you?" Ellie asked.

"You mean the one who was in the news for years? The one with the pervert father. Of course I know of her. What I don't know is why you are interested in her.

"I cannot explain why but it is extremely important that I get in touch with her. I realize it is not your responsibility to do this kind of thing but more than anyone I trust you to find her quickly. We genuinely need your help."

This was more like it. She wanted to be needed. Her instincts told her to hold out for a bit of revenge: a demand for an apology, a statement of outrage or at least a pert comment. The request to find Kat was alluringly appealing, however. There were people she could call. People who knew these things or knew how to get them. She could direct an inquiry. That sounded right smart, she thought. She would make short work of this.

Further, Ellie would owe her. That was worth a great deal. Even better, she would not permit Ellie to return the favor, leaving Ellie forever in her debt. Feeling a bit puffed up by that thought she responded, "I shall find the means for you to contact her as quickly as possible." Dignity intact, she swiftly turned on her heels and left.

When she was gone Ellie told me that her early morning confab with Rita had produced no new information. Rita had left the farewell dinner in a huff because Vince omitted mention of her in his dinner speech while naming virtually everyone else in the office. Vince's slight had so upset her that the rest of the dinner was a blur.

Hardly suspicious behavior on her part.

"Why did you ask her to find Kat for us? She is so touchy and unpredictable." I thought it would be a waste of time. I knew that Rita would not have helped if I had asked.

"I know, she is sensitive and gets her feelings hurt easily, however she has contacts she can reach out to. These people keep track of celebrities, like a fan club. They know where the famous live and what they are doing. If anyone knows where Kat is, it is one of them. And, when it comes to digging into problems Rita is relentless. She will not give up. I'm serious, I trust her more than anyone to help us."

"What happens if she does find Kat? Kat probably wants nothing to do with us. She may have psychological issues after what she's been through. Hell, she may even be unstable. Who knows how she felt about Sam? What if she thinks Sam could have done more to help her and her father? People have killed for less than that." Here we go again I thought. "Does it seem to you that every time we eliminate a suspect we add another?"

Before she could answer, Paul knocked on Ellie's door and entered her office. "Say, glad you two are here. I remembered an odd bit; just popped into my head. I was thinking about Neal after we spoke" (he gestured to me) "and was reminded of him receiving gifts at the dinner. He accepted those gifts as if they were a tribute due to him. Caesar himself would have been more appreciative. He is the most self-centered..."

I motioned for him to get on with his story.

"OK, here is the bit: I think there was one gift missing. Before the dinner, Sam gave a server a package which was taken away. I assumed it was a gift for Neal and would be returned when the gifts were being opened. It wasn't. Perhaps it was for someone else. In any event, I wanted to mention it. Seemed a bit odd in view of what happened later. Good luck inspectors, I hope you get your man."

We considered the implications of this information.

"I had hoped we were finished with the Crown."

"What's wrong with it? I like my pub."

Ellie gave me a knowing smile, "Let's say I could use a change."

Chapter Seventeen

A short distance west from the Toll House the waters of the Regents Canal spread themselves into a pond-sized body of water called Browning's Pool. Restaurants, pubs and retail shops dot its perimeter. Off-center in Browning's Pool lies a small island. Willows shading its shores seem to realize that their purpose, like that of the island, is purely scenic. Their drooping branches decorate the water's edge.

The human pace is easy and relaxed. Passengers are ferried in slow-moving narrow boats from the Pool all the way to Camden Town. The return trip against the weak current lulls tired visitors into a state of lethargy. Heads nod on the final leg of the journey.

Paddington Station, surrounded by a complex of apartments and office buildings, is within sight of the Pool. Its human swarm of activity is seen but not felt in the almost bucolic setting beside the Canal where water fowl outnumber pedestrians.

A man sat outside a waterfront cafe overlooking Browning's Pool. Row boats and small motorized dinghies available for rent bobbed to his right. He waved the waiter over and asked to have his tea refreshed. He had chosen a pleasant day to relax. The sky was overcast however the temperature was mild, very comfortable for sitting outside. A perfect setting to think clearly. The tea sharpened his thoughts. What he had done was in the past. It was now time to concentrate on what he must do. He had recognized her immediately, the girl who reminded him of his mother. He'd almost lost his breath in fact. The moment had passed safely for him but she was a serious threat who must be dealt with. His life had not been easy. His dreams and fantasies had never come true but when his mother had been removed his life began to change. With her gone he had begun to build the life he dreamed of. The pieces were falling into place. No one could be allowed to destroy that. No one.

He needed a plan. Not a partial, ill-conceived one like last time; this time there was no margin for error. He must allow for people doing the unexpected. Above all, he must protect himself. This was self-defense, not fantasy. A preemptive strike.

A loaded ferry arrived from Camden Town. The first unsteady passenger stepped off the boat; the remainder, still drowsy, queued slowly behind her. Soon the sidewalks would be full and then, just as quickly, peace would return.

'Preemptive strike' had sounded good at first. It wasn't. It confused his thinking. This was not a military action. It was a plan to kill another human being before she got to him. It wasn't preemptive, it was premeditated.

Regardless of the semantics, dead was dead. A dead child did not return, no matter how much he prayed. He imagined death was like a black hole, whatever came its way disappeared into it forever. A presence — loved, hated or hardly known — was abruptly gone, just like that.

No stranger to him, he had felt death do its work. He had experienced its transformative power. Before his eyes it had changed that screamer into a perfect angel. His fearful mother into a silent memory. That was then. Circumstances had changed. This time there would be no transformation. Just death. It would be fast and almost painless. An end of life, nothing more.

He must act before she remembered him. A careful, detailed and well thought-out plan would do the job. He should begin at the end. With a clear vision of how the final scene should look, he could easily work backwards. The end determined the means.

First, this was no angel. No restful, serene pose for her. She was his enemy — a threat to the new life he had begun, a reminder of one he had ended. Yet, there must be a clear indication of the relationship between her death and the girl's — after all they were definitely related. There must be a visible connection, a sign to point the way, a signature. Canal side, that was certain. A second canal side death would assuredly get their attention. They couldn't miss that clue. Something more was needed though: another tie to the girl. With two signs they would know it was not a coincidence (it was like leaving a calling card). He would dare them to catch him. He had remained out of the public eye long enough. It was time for him to claim his place. Tantalize them with clues but nothing they could trace to him. Something more...something unique...Of course, it was so obvious. She should be shoeless! They would find a crumpled body, nothing new with that. But a body beside the canal without shoes! A second time. It was genius, a pattern he could repeat.

Now that the scene was set, how to do it? The logistics must be simple but faultless. No, wait. He was jumping forward. He needed to work backwards and not lose his head. The next step was how to get the body canal side. Same as last time, in his car trunk. A detail no one would be aware of but it was important to be consistent. The car ride must be kept short, too many things could go wrong with a car trip from central London. My God! What if there was a traffic stop? The boat rental, practically at his feet as he sipped his tea, would be a short, safe drive. Late at night the area would be dark and quiet. He could take a rowboat without anyone knowing and return it easily. He'd load her into it from his car trunk then row to the Toll House where he would put her canal side. So simple.

Now he must decide how. The options were few since there must be no sound. Consistency is always important but it would be difficult to strangle her. This was a full grown woman not a child, a woman who would struggle, possibly make noise and try to escape. No, this time there would be no strangulation.

A knife would be certain and quiet. Quick too as he already knew. No screaming. Probably a knife then. Certainly a knife, this was no time for indecision.

Yes, a knife.

Chapter Eighteen

Ellie ran into my office without the usual rap on the door. Holding her purse and jacket she said, "Let's go."

I looked at the clock on my computer screen. It was 2:30 pm.

"Now? Leave work now?"

"I will explain it to Vince on the way out. Grab your coat."

"Give me two minutes. I have a couple of things I have to wrap up. Seriously, two minutes..."

"Right. I will be in with Vince, then meet me down in the lobby." She started to leave but turned back, "Can you believe it? Rita found Kat for us."

I made a few quick calls and waited for her in the lobby, surprised that she wasn't there before me. The elevator doors opened minutes later and Ellie stormed out, "Bloody stupid male! He started to lecture me like a school girl, 'Let's not forget that we have a business to run.' He went on and on. I listened for a few minutes then I said, 'Bollocks! You know perfectly well that the business won't suffer without us for a half day. Now is NOT the time for you to act the role of corporate manager, now is when you need to be a person. One who cares about the people around him. A coworker was killed or have you forgotten?' I believe I frightened him. He simply looked at me with his mouth open."

"Good speech!"

Ellie smiled through her anger, "I know, it was awfully good, wasn't it?"

We had passed through the front doors. Outside the weather was damp, wet without raining.

"Where to?" I asked.

"Rita's contact knew where Kat works but not where she lives. According to her Kat teaches a fitness class in St John's Wood in a very trendy athletic club. I know that trainers' schedules are irregular but let's hope she is working today. It is Monday after all which I understand is the busiest day for these clubs. We can use the Underground to go there."

I dreaded riding the Tube in the summer when the humidity was high. Warm weather inevitably transmitted itself underground where the warmth settled and became a pool of heat on the platforms and trains. Coupled with the dampness it would be seriously uncomfortable. I suggested that we take a taxi instead.

"Would you mind if we walked?" she countered. "We can use the extra time to prepare for Kat. As you said, she may not welcome a conversation with us."

Our route took us to Regent's Park, past the Boating Lake, on a foot bridge over the Canal and finally up St John's Woods High

Street to the club. An hour's discussion while walking there had not made us confident about engaging with Kat.   We had developed some ideas and were determined to try, however.

The club's receptionist said that Kat was in the club today but she was currently leading a class. If we would care to wait he promised to tell us when the class was over and we could go on through.

I had noticed a Lamborghini parked outside on the street, flanked by a pair of high-end Mercedes. It seemed decadent for those fine automobiles to be parked on the street like common cars. I tried to guess who their owners might be. Whenever women and men crossed the lobby going to or from the locker room I sized them up. The women all wore similar fashionable workout clothes making it difficult to distinguish a Lamborghini owner amongst them. I thought I had spotted a man who might be the owner because he seemed more interested in the women than in exercise but he went behind the counter at the snack bar and waited on a pair of women after their workout. Unless they were very generous tippers the price of a Lamborghini was beyond his reach.

"I expected more," I whispered to Ellie. "With the kind of money parked outside I expected chandeliers and caviar in the snack bar."

"It is the clientele which is posh not the facilities. The monthly dues cost more than our flats. It keeps out the riff-raff, you know."

After another ten minutes the receptionist told us Kat's cycling class was over and motioned where we should find her. We thanked him and entered a large, open gym filled with exercise equipment. To one side were three rooms. They were open with glass walls separating them from the gym. Floor-to-ceiling mirrors covered their remaining walls. In one room a yoga class was in session. In the cycling room two dozen stationary bikes faced the front of the room. As if confronting them the instructor's bike faced the opposite direction.

While the class filed out the door to the back the instructor remained on her bike staring at the floor in front of her and continued to pedal. We waited for the last of the class to leave. I put my head in the room.

"Kat?"

She slowly raised her eyes to mine but didn't respond.

"Are you Kat? We were friends of Sam. If you are Kat we'd like to talk with you."

During our walk to the club we had decided to open with Sam's name to get an initial reaction from Kat. That reaction would be our clue for how best to proceed.

There was not a flicker of a reaction, she continued to pedal.

"Who are you?"

I told her our names and said that we worked with Sam.

She looked past me. "Ellie, you are Ellie?"

Ellie nodded, "Did Sam mention me to you Kat?"

She stopped pedaling but stayed on the bike. I don't know what I expected Kat to look like. Maybe more like Sam. Maybe slender and girlish. Frightened or damaged. She was none of those things.

Kat looked tough, strong, ready to kick ass.

We let her take her time. We had agreed not to rush her.

She began pedaling again, slowly and deliberately.

She looked at me and asked, "Who are you? Don't tell me your name again and I don't care that you worked with her. Who are you?"

I was confused for a moment, then it came to me.

"Yes, I see what you mean. You are right, I was more than a coworker. Sam was my girlfriend."

This finally got a reaction. Getting off the bike she turned off the music in the room. In the sudden quiet she said to me, "Sam was my girlfriend, too."

It sounded like a plea, not a statement. A plea not to intrude on her memory of Sam.

"I am so sorry for you. I know how it feels," I said. "Sam was a special woman."

For a moment Kat's face softened, "She told me of you last week. Not your name, only that you were part of her life. You are not like I pictured. I don't know what I pictured. Not you. I don't know. I don't know anything." She turned the music on and went back to the bike. "Why are you here? What do you want?"

Ellie answered for me by asking how she learned of Sam's passing.

"What does it matter? She is gone. That is all that matters."

"It's important to us. We want to know what happened to Sam so the police can arrest whoever is responsible."

She jumped off the bike. "The police? Those bastards? They don't care. Likely they are happy she is gone." Both Ellie and I stepped back as Kat advanced. "You want to know how I found out? The police called me. Not to comfort me for losing the woman I loved but to accuse me. That's how I found out. Where was I on the night she was murdered? Would my roommate confirm it? The same people who destroyed my father now were pretending to care about Sam. I know better. Do not ask me to help you with the police. I will not!"

Her anger burst out. The bike nearest to her was sent crashing into the bike next to it. Ellie stepped between her and the next bike she was taking aim at.

"Out of my way! I don't need the help of the police or you or him." She pointed my direction. "I know who killed Sam. I don't need the help of anyone! Leave me alone. Would everyone just leave me alone?"

Ellie did not move. Kat moved threateningly towards her while Ellie held her ground. I was a couple of steps to the side and quickly stepped in to intercept Kat. With a look Ellie told me not to. They were almost toe to toe when Ellie simply opened her arms. Kat hesitated then turned away. Undeterred, Ellie quietly said, "Kat, please, know that I loved her, too."

Kat seemed frozen in place. We waited. Finally, I said, "No police. If you know who did it I promise you I will see to it that he hurts no one else, ever, no matter what." I backed away giving her plenty of room, worried that she might feel cornered.

She looked grateful for the additional space or maybe she was glad to have a private moment with Ellie because she turned back to face her. I couldn't hear what they said. While they talked people slowly began to enter the room and mount their bikes, another exercise class was about to begin. I saw Ellie open her arms and this time Kat accepted the hug. Loud music filled the room before Kat took her place at the front of the class. I followed Ellie out, back to the reception area.

Kat had asked us to wait. This was her last class for the day.

"Do you believe her, that she knows who did it?" I asked.

"I don't know. She is in such a state. I don't know what to think. She said she doesn't want help but I believe she needs it badly."

"That was brave of you to stand up to her like you did."

"Not really. I don't believe she can hurt anyone. She knows too well how it feels. Did you mean it when you said we'd leave the police out of it?"

"I did. Like I told you last night, I want revenge for what he did. I don't want to put it in someone else's hands. And, I don't want to wait. I can't handle a lengthy legal process. The courts may ensure justice but they don't provide satisfaction. Revenge does. I'm not sure that Kat actually knows the person who did it, but if there is a chance that she does, I want first shot at him before the police get to him."

Ellie didn't sit still while we waited. She couldn't. Our encounter with Kat had clearly upset her. She looked out the windows, nosed around the snack bar and stared at her phone but didn't speak. Her thoughts were elsewhere.

I attempted to bring her back, "Had you guessed that Kat was Sam's lover before this?"

"When you first told me about her connection to Sam I wondered. It wasn't until you introduced me and she reacted to my name that I knew for certain."

"You noticed that she did not recognize my name when I introduced us, only yours?"

She nodded.

"And that Sam had only recently told her about me?"

Again she nodded and added, "That doesn't necessarily..."

"Yes, it does. It means she had made her choice and that she chose Kat. I wonder when she planned to break it to me. I suppose I should be hurt but I'm not. After all, she is gone, nothing can change that, and I can see how much she meant to Kat."

A television hung on the wall in the reception room tuned to a sports channel. Highlights of the week's English League games were being shown, replayed and analyzed by commentators.

I wanted to have a replay, a do-over, a second chance to talk to Sam and know her better. I wasn't jealous that Kat had been Sam's choice. I was jealous that Kat had known Sam better than I did.

Chapter Nineteen

His plan had to be thrown out at the last minute, part of it at least. His new one was much, much better. He had seen her package in the pub office and opened it. A pair of red shoes, like the ones his Mum wore when she worked. Nights in his special little room where he must stay quietly. His bed cozy with soft blankets and pillows piled around him. He curled in the warmth and the safety of darkness. Aware that above him coats and jackets hung, like family members looking over him, invisible in the dark but protective.

Once, only once, he cried out. Mum beat him. Never do that again! If you do, you will be out on the street. Understand? Never again.

When he was older and Mum worked less, she said he could sleep in the big room some nights but he refused. The special room was safe, although becoming too small for him. He made himself into a tighter ball and buried his head under the covers.

Momentarily his childhood flashed at the sight of the red shoes. He felt a burst of hatred. The shoes would complete the death scene perfectly and, even better, they gave him the opportunity to get her alone.

He waited until the dinner party ended to speak to her. Everyone had left the room except their boss and the guest of honor. He took her aside and explained that her gift had been taken in error from the pub's office by one of the customers. He wanted her to know that the chap was on his way back to return it in a few minutes. If she wouldn't mind waiting for him outside the back door in ten minutes he would have it for her.

She didn't want to leave without the shoes she bought for Kat (who would look so amazing in them). However, it would be foolish to wait for him by the back door where it was dark. She had told Kat she thought she recognized him but it had been so many years and she wasn't sure.

She decided to meet him in front of the pub, on the street, where it would be safe. Worried that his plan might unravel, he agreed and slipped into the office to get the package. Perhaps he could use it to lure her to the alley where his car was waiting.

Her forgotten purse lay on the desk. An idea formed. He waited ten minutes and met her in front. She was alone, the two men with her had left in a taxi after she told them not to wait. As cars passed, he tried to be as nonchalant and relaxed as possible. "I found this inside. I believe it is your purse. Please check that everything is in it. The bloke should be here any minute with your package."

After checking it, she held the purse close to her, staring him in the eye, "I think I remember you, you know." He played along. Who? Couldn't be him, he explained. He was not that kind of man. At the time of 'that business' he worked in France for an uncle in Lyon. Not in England when it happened, must be a mistake.

She seemed unsure. He continued, he had read about it of course. Even the papers in France covered it. Such a tragic case.

He reached into his pocket for his phone as if he had received a text alert. Pretending to read it he told her, "Ah, says he left it inside the back door. Stay here, be back with it in a moment." Down the alley he hurried. She heard him call out to her, "I believe this is it, Miss." She saw him returning, holding the package out for her. She stepped around the side of the building to take it from him. When he handed her the package, he took her life.

His car was less than twenty feet away. He managed to pull her to it. She was heavier than the child had been yet he was able to lift her into the trunk and carry out the rest according to plan. He drove to the boat rental and with some difficulty got her in the boat. After rowing past the Toll House and dumping her in the bushes he tossed the red shoes in her direction. At the last moment before throwing her purse into the canal he decided to remove the wallet with all its cash and credit cards. He flung it now in the shrubs to show them he was not a common thief; he was not that kind of man.

Chapter Twenty One

Sweaty, tired people made their way to the showers. Carrying a gym bag Kat followed them from the gym and gestured for us to come with her into an office inside the front door. The office was furnished with a small conference table in the middle of the space and a smaller workstation in the corner. We sat around the table.

"I guess I could use your help," Kat said in opening. Her head was down, her eyes were closed. "Actually, I need your help. I know who murdered Sam but I don't know where he is. And you do." We waited for her to continue.

"Sam and I had a bit of an...issue...when she told me about you." Her eyes remained closed as she continued, "I tried to be under-standing but I was truly hurt. She brought me things to make me feel better - cards with sappy sayings, little gifts, notes...you understand. They did help; I loved her more every day. This week she got the odd notion to buy very nice clothes for me. I told her to take them back but it made her feel better to give me gifts she said. She was having fun. Just being Sam. She wanted to take me to a nice restaurant and for me to dress 'to the nines.' Sam made a booking at the restaurant for our big dinner.

"On Thursday, the day before our planned dinner, she called me from the office. She said, 'I have one more gift for you, something you would never buy, to complete your ensemble for our night on the town...sexy hi-heels! I cannot wait to see you in them.' I could picture us, her in her Doc Martins and me in hi-heels. Then she added, 'I think I found the man.' I knew who she meant of course: the man we saw abduct our classmate. The one no one believed us about. We had talked about how someday we would find him. We both believed we would. She said she thought it was him but she wasn't sure. This was on Thursday, the day she was killed."

Kat's eyes had remained closed while she spoke, until now.

"He killed her. He took my only true friend. I want him dead."

***

We gave her a few minutes. I shared her feelings but knew that was the last thing she wanted to hear from me. Sometimes you are protective of your pain because it is all you have.

Ellie broke the silence, "You said Sam called you on Thursday, the day she died?"

Kat looked at Ellie and nodded. She seemed emotionless. Her only loss of composure, when she was throwing bikes around, was when we mentioned the police. Otherwise she was in control of her feelings which surprised me. I think I had expected her to be shaken and passive; a victim. Instead she was surprisingly strong. Maybe being a victim as a young girl had toughened her or maybe she had always been this way, an anchor, attractive to Sam because she could be relied on.

"So that day was the first time she had seen the man since the day of the abduction?" Ellie asked.

"This is where I need your help. Sam had in fact seen him several times before Thursday. At first she thought it might be him. It had been years and she wanted to be more confident before she told me. Didn't want to get my hopes up if she was wrong. She said each time she saw him she became more inclined to believe it was him."

"This man, did she say what his name is?"

"It wouldn't have meant anything to me, all I knew was his face. It is a face I cannot forget. I must find him. Sam said she was with you at your pub when she saw him." She slid her chair closer to me. "I simply need for you to tell me where your pub is."

"Someone at the pub? We suspected the people at our dinner but if it could have been any of the pub's customers..."

"Not 'any' customer, only regulars that Sam would have seen more than once at the pub in the last few weeks," Ellie corrected me.

"I will know him when I see him. Tell me where the pub is, please."

"Better than that, we will take you."

"I prefer to go alone."

"No chance. What if he recognizes you? He's a killer. You can't go alone. No way. Ellie and I will be with you. Let's go right now. Do you need to change clothes or anything?"

"I would like to clean up. I have been do-ing classes all afternoon. Give me the address then you go on. I will be there shortly and join you."

Ellie replied "How about if I wait for you here while he goes on to the pub?"

She agreed, a little reluctantly, but her evasions hadn't worked and she knew from Ellie's tone that she had no choice.

I left them at the gym. Outside, the damp weather had not improved. I made a few phone calls before leaving High Street. The walk from St. John's Wood to Little Venice was not far. I considered using a route that would take me past the famous Abbey Road crossing but the one by Lord's Cricket Ground was more direct. Cheers from the stadium indicated that a match was in progress which meant there would be large crowds at the Crown only a half dozen blocks away.

The bistro tables in front were overflowing when I arrived. Empty pint glasses filled the tables, surrounded by male cricket fans in their club ties. Judging by their level of relaxation many had left the match early. The men stood in groups around the tables, some swaying slightly, others using the tables for stability. I felt sorry for Will. This would be a long night for him.

The first person I saw when I went inside was Hugh. He jumped up from his booth when he caught sight of me. "Christ man, so sorry about Sam. Damned awful. Come, sit here with me. I have a booth. I was hoping to see you. Tell me, can I get a beer for you?" He was back with a pint in a flash.

I sat on the side of the booth where I could watch the front door.

Hugh sounded and looked sincere but of course he would if he were involved wouldn't he? I played it straight, hoping to get him to talk. I asked when he heard about Sam's murder.

"Friday noon. The police were all over my boat. They knew I had joined your dinner group for a bit of chatter so when they learned I live on a boat mere blocks away they decided to come say hello. Weren't at all happy when I told them I came directly back to the boat after leaving the pub. Alone. No alibi. How about you? Did they advise you not to leave London too?"

"They did, for many of the same reasons."

"I thought it best to spend the weekend at Susan's flat. Didn't want the neighbors bothered if the police chose to call on me again."

"We learned something about Sam today, Hugh. Something that I was unfamiliar with but seems to be common knowledge of Londoners." He listened attentively. "When she was younger Sam and a girl named Kat were involved in an infamous case where their schoolmate was snatched. Kat's father was believed to have been involved. I'm told it was all over English TV and newspapers at the time."

"Sam was involved in that business? I had no idea. Tragic situation. I always wondered about the parents of the girl who was abducted. Their little girl taken from them but everyone only talked about Kat and her father."

"Sam's murder may be related to that case. Whether it is or not, I want to find this guy and even the score."

"Quite right, an eye for an eye I say. The dead should be revenged. They deserve it. Legal niceties be damned! ."

"Unlike you, not many people share my feelings in this regard."

"I lost my wife and daughter to a drunk driver years ago. Two years in jail was his sentence. Two years! He was out before I was done grieving. Does that sound like justice?"

"How old was your daughter?"

Hugh thought for a few moments. "She would be twenty-six. Same as Sam."

Maybe it was just me, but why compare their ages?

The crowd of cricket fans grew. Behind the bar, Thomas was trying to keep up with demand. He was not at his best with a rowdy male crowd where his charm and good looks didn't make up for being slow and rather careless with drink orders. Two men were complaining loudly that he had given them the wrong drinks. He argued that those were exactly the drinks they had ordered which set off other customers who took up their cause. The situation might have escalated but Will came from the office in back and set matters straight by sending Thomas to collect empty glasses while giving the two men free drinks.

Although badly outnumbered, there were women in the pub too. In the booth next to ours were three women. I recognized them from a small gallery on Edgware Road. Two were co-owners, the third a sales associate. At least that is what was printed on their name tags the day Sam and I went into the gallery. I had been drawn to a series of watercolors on display in the window. They were laughably expensive but we had looked around at other paintings when told the price as if money was not a concern. We thought we pulled it off admirably. I'm sure we fooled no one.

Thomas approached their booth, ostensibly to take away their empties, however it was obvious that they were flirting with him and that he preferred their company to the rowdy lads at the bar.

Hugh leaned across the table, "He is quite the ladies man, that Thomas."

"Women do seem to find him attractive. Do you know him at all outside the pub?"

"Not really. I know he likes the ladies and fishing. Usually anglers are a more sensible lot," Hugh laughed.

"Any idea when he moved here from Australia?"

"None. He has been working at the pub since I bought the boat and mooring here a year after my wife and daughter were taken. I needed a change of scene."

Rita and Paul had come through the door. I waved them over to join us. Thomas stopped talking to the gallery ladies when he saw them. Hugh acted nervous. "Your friends from the dinner?" He asked me.

Rita ignored him. "We got your message and brought a taxi here. Where are they and why are all these club ties here?"

"Not here yet and cricket match at Lord's."

"I detest uniforms, " began Paul, "they are more inane than dress codes. You Americans are on the right track with your 'casual attire.'

Should take it farther, wear what one likes as long as the privates are covered. Why these nobs voluntarily dress alike at a sports event makes no sense to me. None at all."

Rita resumed, "Not here yet? Why the bloody hell did we have to rush about to come quickly?"

I told her to hold her horses (a phrase that caused her to wince) while I called Ellie to find out where they were.

"Kat and I are about two blocks away."

"Is everything OK? I expected you to arrive by now. I called Paul and Rita to meet us. They are here with me now. As are Hugh and Thomas."

"Oh, right. We are doing well now, I will explain. Do us a favor and meet us outside but ask the others to wait inside."

I did as requested although Rita was clearly unhappy being left with Hugh and Paul. I asked Paul to entertain them with his views regarding why he refused to watch legal dramas on television while I went outside. He had launched into a zesty spiel against courtroom theatre before I left the booth.

Ellie and Kat were across the street waiting in the twilight for the traffic light to change. Kat wore tights, athletic shoes and a sweatshirt. I thought Paul would approve.

She apologized when they crossed the street. "All my fault. A small panic attack back there when I realized I was about to face him. Is he in there?"

"You will have to tell us. The men who we think are suspects are inside. Hopefully you will see the one you are looking for. If you do see him don't do anything, OK? Simply tell us. With all these cricket fans here he probably won't notice you so there is no reason for us to hurry. Once you identify him we will decide what to do. We will decide as a group. Do you agree?"

She looked scared as she nodded.

"You can do this, Kat," Ellie reassured her.

"I know, I know."

"I think it would be better for Ellie and I to go in before you. There is less chance of you being recognized if you are not with us. Wait a few minutes. When you come in, look around the bar like you are looking for someone waiting for you. Take your time. Keep looking around after you see him, then go outside. That will be our signal. We will follow you out and determine what steps to take. Remember, you are not alone. We all want to get this guy."

She looked relieved that there would not be a confrontation. Ellie suggested that she go next door to the grocery store and buy candy or gum to give us time to get inside and take our place in the booth. We watched her enter the store.

Inside the market, Kat tried to kill time by walking down the food aisles. This was it, she thought. The man who had taken so much from her was finally going to pay for what he had done. It was long overdue and made her heart race to think about it. She was both frightened and elated. If only Sam was here to share this with her.

After paying for a candy bar, which she had no intention of eating, she thought she caught a glimpse of a man watching her from the end of an aisle. Could it be him? How could he know she was there? She decided to confront him but when she got there he was gone.

***

"Do you still believe her story?" I said to Ellie while Kat was in the store.

"Her panic attack was real. She was terrified of seeing him. Yes, I most certainly believe her."

"Well, lets hope he is inside."

Rita and Paul were alone in the booth when we entered. "Where's Hugh?" I asked.

"Said he needed to powder his nose. Paul's theory of cinematic subjects drove him to a pee I believe. Where is the famous Kat?"

"This is not a celebrity sighting," I reminded Rita. Ellie explained our plan to Paul and her. We would watch for Kat and when she left we would all leave.

Hugh returned, still looking uneasy. "Please tell me, what's doing?"

"Work discussion. How to cover Sam's job, you know."

I doubt that he believed me however he let us take his booth and stood at the bar. Thomas had moved on from the gallery women, picked up a tray of empty glasses and joined the man in the brown sweater who had just taken a seat on the opposite side of the bar.

The door opened. First I saw Stephen gallantly trying to hold it open for someone. Then I saw Kat. Holding the door wasn't going so well for Stephen - it was heavier than he was and shut despite his efforts. He pulled it open; it threatened to close again, pulling him sliding and swearing behind. Kat interceded, grabbed the door and pushed him in ahead of her. The cricket fans near the door thought this was humorous but I knew that the reason Kat did it was to shield her face behind him.   Once inside Stephen turned to make a gentlemanly bow to her but Kat was gone.   She had swiftly moved behind a loud group in club ties. Stephen gave up looking for her, saw Hugh at the bar and joined him. I tried to keep an eye on them while watching Kat.

Hugh occasionally glanced over to our booth while listening to Stephen. I guessed he was telling Hugh how Val had cornered him and made him talk.   Sure enough Hugh left him at the bar and started over to our booth to ask for an explanation, I assumed.

Meanwhile Kat had continued to study the faces in the pub. She had done as I asked, acting like she was looking for a specific friend, until moments before Hugh came towards the booth.   Then she seemed to panic. She came around the bar and came straight for our booth, making it there before Hugh. "I lost him. I think he recognized me and made a run for it. He's gone!"

"Who is it?"

"I told you I don't know his bloody name. The guy at the bar."

I pointed to Hugh who now was standing with us at the booth, "Him?"

"Do you think I'm stupid? I can see him can't I? No, it was the other guy."

I turned her in the direction of Thomas, working behind the bar, "Him?"

She gave me a withering look, "Good Christ! No! He must have gone out the back door." She stepped quickly to the office behind the bar and disappeared through the door to the hallway on the side of the pub. I knew if we all followed her through the office everyone in the pub would know something was up so I told Ellie to come with me out the front door. "Rita and Paul, wait for us here. You come too, Hugh. I will explain as we go."

Outside night had fallen. We turned down the alley beside the pub. Although it was dark we could see Kat giving chase to someone running ahead. She was already more than a block from us. The person she pursued was nearly to the towpath by the canal.

I explained to Hugh that the woman running was Kat and the person she was chasing was the person she said was Sam's killer and that I would welcome his help. "Wouldn't miss it for the world," as he joined in the chase.

In the streetlight I could see that Kat was gaining on the person who had turned onto the tow path and was running in the direction of the Toll House. Kat was a strong runner but had a lot of distance to make up. We ran as fast as we could, worried what might happen if Kat did catch him.

Chapter Twenty Two

His legs felt like jello. Not since his teens had he run more than a few yards at a time. Now he was running for his life and this demon threatened to catch him. After running as fast as he could for three blocks he was hardly able to breathe and yet she had not slowed at all. He realized he could not outrun her when he had gone another block and crossed the bridge by the Toll House. The island in Browning's Pool was his only hope. If he could swim to it surely he would be safe. It was his only hope. The moment he had seen her in the pub he knew it was Kat. He had followed her years ago on television and newspapers where he saw her face daily for months. He knew her and had no doubt that she recognized him. With luck he thought he could slip away from the pub amongst the crowd without her seeing him leave but when he looked back in the alley there she was. Run, he told himself but this devil ran with him.

He stumbled crossing the lawn that lead down to the water, his legs about to collapse under him. The water was cold, his feet heavy as he waded in. When he felt her grab him by the collar and pull him back he was almost re-lieved. He didn't resist. Too tired to swim. No air. He knew he would have drowned.

She pulled and dragged him to the grass, shoved him down face first and straddled his back.

"Do not make a sound," she warned him. "I have a rock in my hand."

He had no breath, he could not have cried out if he wanted. She pulled his hands behind his back.

He did not try to move. He made no noise. He waited.

***

Hugh and I had lost track of them until we heard splashing from Browning's Pool. By the time we got to the lawn Kat already had him under control. We ran over to help her although she obviously didn't need our assistance. I looked at the face in the grass.

"Will? Are you kidding me? Will?"

"I don't know this bastard's name but he is the pervert who molested my schoolmate and killed her and Sam."

"I did not molest her! I would never do anything like that to her. It was not like that at all. She was to be my daughter. My family. My little angel."

"Then why did you murder her?" Kat snapped, pulling his arms painfully back. He began to yell but she reminded him that she still held the rock.

"Don't hurt me. I won't yell out. I didn't murder her, she died."

"You killed her!"

"The screaming killed her. I didn't want her to die but the screaming was horrible and then she was dead. I took care of her. I put her in a beautiful place by the water. I arranged her hair and made her comfortable. I even removed her wet shoes. It looked like a painting. She looked so beautiful."

"You sick bastard. I suppose you didn't murder Sam either. Were her shoes wet too when you left her barefoot in the shrubbery?"

"No, she was different. She would have put me out on the street. I know she would. I didn't want to kill. I had to. Don't you see? When she was dead she had to be barefoot like the other one. For consistency. And her shoes, they were so ugly but I left those red shoes for her."

"Those shoes were for me you fucker! Sam bought those for me!" Kat's anger exploded, she raised the stone but Hugh and I were able to take it from her before she cracked his skull. She glared at us.

I felt my phone vibrate before it rang. It was Ellie.

"Where the hell is everyone?"

"On the lawn by the island in the Pool. Where are you?"

"On the way to Paddington. Must have passed by you in the dark. I will be there in two minutes, don't leave!"

Kat refused to get off Will. Without the stone she couldn't hurt him badly so we waited for Ellie to help us talk her off him.

"Help me, Hugh," Will pleaded. "We have always been friends. Get her off me. Let me go."

"Help you? If she asks me to I will kill you myself."

"Kill me? What! Why kill me? I never did anything to you."

"You are a killer, the same as the man who killed my wife and daughter. I would not think twice about ending your life."

"I didn't touch them! I never even met your wife and daughter!"

"Consider yourself a proxy for their killer. I would do it without remorse."

"And you? You won't help me?" he pleaded with me.

"You murdered Sam and yet ask me that question?" I answered.

"All I wanted was a family. A daughter who I could tuck into a real bed, in her own room at night, buy presents for and take to the zoo. That's all. I meant no harm. I am a good man. Please let me go. I won't hurt anyone."

I heard Ellie on the sidewalk and called to her. She walked down to the lawn and saw us. "This is him?"

"Not much to look at, is he?" Hugh said.

"Kat, how are you?" Ellie put her hand on Kat's shoulder.

Kat seemed to wilt. "Not like I expected. He is so … pathetic and weak. I wanted someone to hate. I wanted revenge for Sam and my father. I have waited years for this but he is not worth it. He doesn't deserve my hatred. He is nothing more than a sick and warped little man."

Ellie said, "He is not worth it then, but you are. Let the guys take him."

Kat freed his hands but hesitated to stand. Ellie took her arm and helped her up. Standing over him Kat was slow to move. Ellie gave her a moment and still holding her arm guided her away from him. Will made no effort to escape.

"What do you want us to do with him?" Hugh asked Kat.

"I don't care. He is so pitiful. I know I should feel compassion for him but I cannot. I simply want him out of my life. Do whatever you think is best."

Kat seemed spent. She looked once more at Will, still face down on the lawn, then turned her back on him.   Ellie followed Kat as she walked away. She called back to us, "I will see to it that she gets home safely."

I exchanged a glance with Hugh.   We waited until the women were far enough away that they wouldn't hear, then we helped Will to his feet and walked him into the Pool. He wept but seemed to understand it was over and offered little resistance.   When we were chest deep we held him firmly under the waters of the canal until the struggling stopped. He settled to the bottom when we released him.

Then we left, satisfied.

The police could have him now.

Epilogue

The Court of Inquiry ruled Will's death was a suicide. No evidence of physical trauma was found. None of the men with club ties at the pub that evening remembered anything, which was not surprising, few remembered how they got home. Thomas I am sure suspected something but testified at the hearing that Will's behavior of late was erratic. Further, Thomas had discovered irregularities in the finances of the Crown which indicated that Will had taken large sums of money from the pub for his personal use. The police have been unable to determine where the money was spent.

Kat returned to her exercise class the next day to continue with her training job and still lives in her room at the flat of her lazy room-mate. She and Ellie meet for lunch once a week. Experienced as I am with Ellie's relent-less patience I am confident that in time Kat will succumb. Fate dares not mess with Ellie.

Hugh sold his boat and bought a flat near Hampstead Heath. Susan moved in to help him begin to build a new life. I had a pint of ale with him soon after he moved, at a pub by his new flat. It was an awkward affair, neither of us wanting to mention Will or Sam. When we part-ed Hugh said he was done with canal life. I un-derstood that included me.

At a dinner Rita hosted for Val, Ilyse, Paul and the twins she surprised herself by actually beginning to enjoy Paul's contrarian comments. She surprised him by inviting him for dinner by himself at her flat the next weekend. Then for dinner every weekend since. Sometimes he stays over.

I have not bought a narrow boat. There are too many memories associated with canal life for me to possibly own one. I did move to a new flat, closer to Camden Town and farther from the Toll House.

The life of an expat still appeals to me and I am not ready to return to the States just yet despite what happened. The effects remain, however. I frequently awake in the middle of the night and think about the whole affair. I hope that Sam approves of the way it ended. I'm afraid that she may not.

One issue usually prevents me from falling back to sleep. Not the role I played in avenging the lives he took. No, I don't regret that, not a bit. It is the money Will embezzled. Where did it go? News reports about missing children unnerve me. I recall him saying something about a secluded, quiet cottage somewhere in the country.

Printed in Great Britain
by Amazon

41864905R00118